THE
PROTECTLINGS
At Woods Edge

Written and Illustrated by

Carolyn Heilman

Printed in the United States of America
First Printing, 2015
ISBN-10: 0-9862803-2-1
ISBN-13: 978-0-9862803-2-0

Parallel Minds Press
(DBA of Parallel Minds LLC)
332 Goodmans Hill Road
Sudbury, MA 01776
www.parallelminds.com

Cover Illustration Copyright © 2015 by Carolyn Heilman
Book design and production by Parallel Minds Press
Editing by Carol Callahan
Chapter illustrations © 2015 Carolyn Heilman
Author photograph by Steve Robb

For Alex and Erika

CONTENTS

"All things great are wound up with all things little."

L.M. Montgomery
Anne of Green Gables

PROLOGUE

Behind the curtains in the nursery, two tiny pairs of feet shuffled on the windowsill. There was a muffled, mouse-like sneeze. Marta pressed her hands over her mouth and squeezed her eyes shut. Although she felt the tickle of a second sneeze, she held her breath and willed it away. Standing next to Tom on the sill, she could sense his relief. They had been hiding there for hours, waiting for the twins to be put to bed.

Just under six inches tall, Marta and Tom spent most of their time hiding. Away from the safety of their homestead under the old beech tree, Woodlanders had to be careful. They relied on each other in their daily work. The job they came to do tonight was dangerous. The little couple bided their time, restless but patient. They waited, and would continue to wait, as long as necessary.

Unaware of the Woodlanders behind the curtains, Beth Morley gently placed her newborn son in the crib. He protested loudly, crying until his sister was laid beside him. Then, Oliver promptly quieted down and fell asleep. Paige was fussing too, but when her brother relaxed and began breathing deeply, she settled down to sleep as well. Their parents stepped away slowly. They watched the twins' chests rise and fall as they slept.

"Aren't they perfect?" Beth sighed to her husband. Paul nodded and yawned. Oliver and Paige were glowing with good health and full hearts. Beth admired them fondly, then sensed some movement out of the corner of her eye, by the window. Tiredly dismissing her curiosity, she took Paul's hand and tiptoed out of the room. They silently closed the door behind them.

Tom smiled at Marta as he stepped out from behind the curtains. He breathed in the clean scents of soap and baby powder. The twins were precious. He sighed, and reached out a hand to Marta, helping her to the edge of the sill.

"Will they do?" he asked with hopeful eyes. Taking his hand, Marta stepped off the sill and onto the narrow edge of the crib. Squeezing between the slats, she sat down on the soft bedding printed with fuzzy ducks. As she looked at the rosy faces of the sleeping twins, her heart warmed. Oliver and Paige were, indeed, perfect. She took a deep breath and placed her elbows on her knees, resting her chin in her hands.

"Yes," she smiled. "They'll do."

MARCH

In the woods, dusk was settling. After a long week at the Morley's, Marta and Tom were looking forward to a good night's rest. That would have to wait. This meeting of the Woodlanders in the Great Hall deep beneath the roots of the ancient beech tree was necessary but would not take long.

Marta's father, Walter, approached the podium. At a full seven inches he was a tall Woodlander, an imposing figure. His green eyes were bright and intense, his posture straight and determined. As a leader he was greatly respected and adored. A slight elevation of chin and brow was all that was needed to get everyone's attention. He waited patiently for things to quiet down. After all, it was an exciting event and they had been waiting for weeks to hear the news. His wife, Elsa, smiled and nodded from the front row where she was saving him a seat.

"Good evening, my fellow Woodlanders," Walter bellowed. "Please quiet down so that we can begin. I know we're all eager to hear Marta and Tom's report on their recent expedition to Woods

Edge." Walter turned to face his daughter and son-in-law, seated next to him in front of the crowd.

While the Woodlanders settled into their seats, Tom rose from his chair next to Marta and shook Walter's hand. He tried to return his huge smile, but came up short. Walter sat down next to Elsa and reached over to hold her hand.

Tom hated speaking in front of a crowd. It made him nervous, causing his stomach to lurch and rumble. He was sure everyone could hear the gurgling noises. Usually, Marta reviewed the reports with him. She was good at that, very relaxed and at ease. Tonight she was exhausted from their trip, having missed a night's sleep. Tom wanted her to rest. He looked out at the eager faces and took a deep breath.

"Hello everyone," Tom's voice rang out, cracking a little. He turned to Marta and blinked. She smiled over at him, boosting his confidence instantly. He took a deep breath and faced the crowd.

"Marta and I just returned this morning from Woods Edge." Tom swallowed loudly. "As you all know from our previous expedition several months ago, we were following up on the babies due at the Morley home on Primrose Lane." He felt a bead of sweat dripping down his forehead and hoped no one could see it.

"To briefly review that past report, Beth and

Paul Morley scored extremely well in all areas of testing." Tom turned to face a large poster of the parents' test scores next to the podium. The crowd murmured with approval and excitement. "We can predict with confidence that these children will be raised with care and attention to their well-being."

Tom continued. "We are extremely lucky to have twins available. Marta and I looked over the records to find that it has been fourteen years since we last trained twins. I'm sure you all remember Cara and Cody MacKenzie ..." Hums of fond recollection buzzed through the crowd.

Tom exhaled deeply, and went on to explain that training would begin in two weeks. As Master Dreamguiders, Tom and Marta would oversee all aspects of educating and training Oliver and Paige Morley. By the arrival of their eighth birthday, the bond between the Woodlanders and the twins would be secure and enduring.

★ ★ ★

On a beautiful spring Saturday evening in the Rawlings Meadow neighborhood, the Penning family was setting the table for dinner. Samantha, age 11, was in charge of silverware and napkins. Her little brother, Jared, put out the plates. It was a big job for a six-year-old, so Samantha helped him. Their mother brought crescent rolls over from the oven and placed them on the table.

"Honey, are the ribs ready?" she called out toward the patio. Their dad nodded to her before lifting the lid of the grill, allowing the smoke to billow into his face. Sputtering, he called to Samantha. "Come and get 'em!" She raced out to give him a hand.

"Dad, you smell like a campfire," teased Samantha. He threw an oven mitt at her, missing by a long shot.

Seated around the table, the four of them joined hands. When his mom asked Jared to say the blessing, he tried on a serious face.

"Thank you for this yummy-smelling food," Jared began. "And thank you for warm weather coming, and my sister's great stories she tells me, and Mum's buttery crescent rolls, and Dad's card tricks, and ..."

"Good job, Buddy," his dad interrupted gently. "Pass those rolls to Jared, will you Sam? I think we are going to need a double stack of napkins," he added, wiggling his fingers at Samantha. She pushed some paper towels in his direction.

"How was your day in the woods, Sam?" her mom inquired between nibbles on a rib. Careful not to give too much information about how she had spent her afternoon, Samantha answered thoughtfully.

"Kinda quiet. The ferns are coming out. It's muddy back there." She looked down at her plate to avoid her mother's gaze.

The woods were behind the Penning's house. Rawlings Meadow was a development of houses with streets named after flowers. Before it became a neighborhood, the area had been a big farm owned by the Rawlings family. The houses were built around hundreds of acres of conservation land. Primrose Lane, where the Pennings lived, backed right up against the woods. Sam felt like she had the biggest backyard in the world.

"Can I come with you tomorrow?" Jared pleaded at her from across the table. For Sam, it was not an option for Jared to accompany her into the woods. But distracting him was easy.

"How about we build a fort on the patio—a hideout for you and Bunny?" Sam pointed to a fifth chair at the table, where Jared's stuffed rabbit sat propped up in front of a plate of lettuce and celery.

"Cool! We can sleep out there in our pajamas.

You and me, and Bunny," he added.

"I'm afraid it's not quite warm enough yet, Jared," his mom shook her head. "Especially at night. The fort can be your Sunday project tomorrow, but you'll have to sleep in your own bed. Deal?" She smiled, encouraging him with another roll.

"Deal!" He snatched one and stuffed the whole thing into his mouth in one bite. Relieved, Sam licked sticky sauce off her fingers.

There was a knock at the kitchen door. Sam knew it would be her best friends, Palmer and Lulu, hoping to get her outside for a game of Creepy Tag, their version of tag in the dark. They would need the last half hour of light to set the boundaries, which changed every time they played.

"Come on in, kids," Sam's mom called out, rising from the table with the plate of leftover rolls. The door swung open, and Palmer and Lulu bounded in, bringing in green scents from the spring evening.

Palmer and Lulu were a year younger than Sam, but they were all in the same grade. Taking two rolls from the plate, Palmer bit into one and stuffed the other into his pocket. Lulu took one as well and stuck her finger through it, wearing it like a ring.

"Beautiful, Mrs. Penning. Thank you very much." Mary Louise—no one called her that; Lulu suited her much better—was small for her age, but had no trouble keeping up with Palmer and Samantha.

Sam's dad stood up and began clearing the table. "Samantha has to do her evening chores first, guys. Give her a minute." He stacked the plates and grabbed a few glasses, heading to the sink. Jared and his mom made their way upstairs with Bunny for stories and a bath.

Sam smiled at her friends, licked her fingers one more time and pushed her chair away from the table.

"I just have to clear up and take out the trash," explained Sam.

"Do you have your watch on?" her dad asked over his shoulder. Sam paused with the trash bag in hand.

"Synchronize," she replied, checking her orange watch.

"It's 6:35 now, be home at 7:30 on the nose," he advised, looking at his own watch.

"Dad, it's Saturday," she replied, trying not to whine. He gave in, and changed his mind.

"Right. 8 then—you'll need a bath."

Sam thanked him with a kiss. Palmer took the trash bag from her and headed out to the garage. Lulu helped her wipe off the table. Then, arm in arm, they headed out into the fading light.

In the yard, darkness began to settle. Palmer set

up the boundaries for Creepy Tag around the house. Samantha and Lulu followed behind him as he numbered off four corners. He chose the garden shed and the big pine tree to mark the limits in the backyard. A lamppost and a mailbox in the front yard completed a big square around the house, with the gate into the woods as base. A round of 'rock, paper, scissors' determined that Lulu would be The Creep, so she headed over to the base, followed by her friends.

Lulu turned around and set her hands on her hips. "Let's make this game creepier—let's play it in the woods." She gazed toward the gate and raised her eyebrows, smiling.

Sam looked at Palmer. She couldn't see his face very well in the dim light, but sensed his hesitation. It matched her own. She was about to say something when Palmer spoke up.

"That would be fun, but we need some light to play." He sounded as though he was considering it, but Sam knew he was not. He added, "It's pitch dark in there, and it would be really hard to set the boundaries."

Sam nodded, pretending she didn't care one way or the other. Lulu sighed.

"Okay," Lulu gave in. "We can think about it for next time. We could use flashlights and bring our bike flags to mark the boundaries. It would be awesome ..." Her voice trailed off as she turned back to the gate and started counting.

Satisfied, Palmer and Sam made their way in the descending darkness to the boundaries in the front yard. They had a few minutes before Lulu would be sneaking up on them.

Sam stopped on the curb next to the mailbox. She watched Palmer pace around the neighbor's lamppost in the next yard. Lulu would choose one of them to chase to the base, and only one player could be on it at a time, for two minutes. Then The Creep would try to tag the kid off base, so it was smart to hide. This was challenging, as The Creep was not always in sight. Often he or she would hide as well. The dark made it hard to tell who was approaching. Sam's heart was already racing.

Lulu finished counting. She shouted from the backyard: "Run for your lives!" Palmer and Sam turned to face the house, looking from one side to the next, and back again, on guard.

Lulu appeared closest to Palmer and stopped. Sam could see her outline, and tried to follow her movements in the shadows from the rising moon. It looked like she was going after Palmer, but it was best to stay alert. Lulu was tricky. She made a step toward Palmer, but then changed direction and sprinted straight for Sam.

Springing into action, Sam made her way toward base, leaping over flowerbeds and racing to the backyard with all her strength. She could hear Lulu gaining on her as she made a beeline for the gate. It was hard to see the path. In huge strides, she was safe, colliding with the wood and bruising her shoulder on the handle. She collapsed against it, gasping to catch her breath.

Turning around, she searched for The Creep, but Lulu had disappeared into the darkness. There was no way to tell if she had gone off to find Palmer, or was waiting in the shadows for Sam's base time to be over. Sam counted to 120 as slowly as she could, scanning the yard for any movement. She wouldn't be able to get on base again until Palmer had his turn there. Her heart was pounding. Spring peepers chirped from the woods. In big gulps, she inhaled the moldy smell of mushrooms that hung around the rotting wooden gate and its stone posts.

Her base time was up. Warily, she stepped away from the gate. Heading to one of the boundaries in the front yard seemed like a good plan. She crept quietly, turning around in circles. Footsteps crunched a twig nearby, and she bolted away from the snapping sound. Running at full speed in the dark made her feel like she was falling. Focusing on the streetlight ahead, she rounded the side of the house and made her way toward it.

Suddenly, she collided with a shadow that stepped out from the bushes. Her feet shot out from under her and she landed flat on her back with a thud. Although the grass was soft, a loud noise rang in her ears. She shook her head to clear it. Lulu's laughter replaced the ringing. She, too, was on her back nearby, giggling.

"Ow!" Lulu whined, still laughing. "We bonked heads! You all right?" Lulu asked her friend, sitting up slowly next to her. Sam began laughing as she nodded, propping herself up on her elbows.

They fell back, cracking up and wheezing, until Palmer appeared. He joined their pileup in the grass and they inhaled the cool night air. Looking up at the stars, their heads rested together on the lawn in the moonlight like the center of a peace sign. It was time to go in, but they lay there quietly, listening to the sounds of nightfall.

APRIL

Deep in the night, the wind howled. Samantha awakened to find herself tangled in her navy blue sheets. A glance at the digital clock on the nightstand confirmed what she already knew: it was midnight. The full moon cast shadows across the floor of her room. It seemed as if streetlights were shining outside her window, but there were none. Her room was at the back of the house, facing the woods where she spent so much of her time. Samantha knew the many acres there as if she had viewed them from high above the trees. She had a map in her mind that included every path, boulder, and stream.

While her classmates in fifth grade played soccer and video games, she preferred the woods. They captivated her attention in every season, since her earliest memories. The fact that most kids had no interest in the woods was fine with her. It made her job much easier. She was a Protectling. The Woodlanders counted on her to keep them safe. It was a heavy secret, but her devotion to them was steady. Even when she had been tempted to tell someone, her tongue would not betray her.

Gathering the clothes she had laid out on her desk, Samantha changed out of her pajamas. The nights were no longer cold, but she had brought up her sweatshirt from downstairs, just in case. A long-sleeved, purple tee shirt and jeans seemed just right. She pulled her long brown hair into a ponytail and tied the sweatshirt around her waist. Her green sneakers had no laces and slipped on quickly. She didn't want to be late.

The wind whistled outside, picking up speed and whipping through the tall trees in the yard. A loud cracking noise brought Sam quickly to the window. A huge branch had fallen onto the patio below. She stood motionless, waiting to see if anyone in the house had been awakened. A few moments of quiet satisfied her.

Samantha enjoyed helping the Woodlanders with their spring chores in the woods. Mostly this included cleaning up after winter: clearing trails, and repairing broken chimneys and stovepipes. Samantha didn't do these jobs for them. They preferred to do the work themselves. Her responsibility was to keep them safe from harm.

She was not alone. There were always a few other Protectlings on the job, mostly kids she knew from town. Samantha enjoyed their company and was always glad to see them, especially Palmer.

Curiously, she never felt the need to talk to him about their work. It was understood that their secrecy was for the safety of the Woodlanders. They never questioned it.

Sam waited a few more cautious moments before opening her window. Lowering the braided ladder that she had retrieved from between her mattress and box spring, she attached its knotted ends to large bolts that were screwed into the window frame. Crafted by herself according to instructions from Marta and Tom, she was certain the ladder could hold her weight. It was sturdy and beautiful, woven out of knotted strips of flannel from her outgrown pajamas and her brother's old play clothes.

Earthy scents rushed in from the night, swirling around her. Climbing carefully through the window, she steadied her feet a few steps down the ladder. Closing the window was a challenge, but she took her time. Stepping down slowly, she landed softly on the patio bricks. She stepped over the fallen branch and made her way toward the back of the yard. With the full moon above, it was easy to see where she was going.

The gate into the woods squeaked loudly as she opened it. Sam winced and closed her eyes, hoping no one inside had heard it. A few moments of silence passed and Samantha sighed with relief. She glanced back at the dark house before moving on.

There were not many after-dark requests from the Woodlanders, but Samantha enjoyed them the most. The woods came alive at night. She knew the different calls of the owls and never grew tired of identifying them. It was always exciting to hear one above in a tree, and to see its round eyes looking down at her.

Just then Samantha heard the hoot of a barred owl: "Who! Who! Who cooks for yooouuuu!" The large bird flew out of a nearby tree and soared off into the night. Her heart raced as she listened to the beat of its huge wings fade into silence.

It wasn't totally quiet. Samantha could hear small animals scurrying about in the underbrush. Mostly, the night creatures would be afraid of her and stay out of her path. One night, she had come upon a sleeping doe and her fawn. The deer sat up at the sound of her footsteps and bolted away, startling her. She was thrilled by the possibility of seeing them again. Walking carefully, she tread as softly as she could. She stepped off the trail and pushed her way through saplings and shrubs.

Up ahead in the moonlight, Samantha spotted the huge beech tree that marked the entrance to the Woodlanders' homestead. It was magnificent. Walter had told her that the tree was over a hundred years old.

Samantha had to make her way through prickly bushes to get to the clearing around the beech tree.

Brambles caught at her jeans, slowing her progress. Finally, her path was clear. She paused for a moment and took in a deep breath. The night air smelled like moss and moist earth.

From behind her came a small chirping sound, along with a rustling in the bushes. She turned around slowly, quietly. There in the moonlight she saw a fat raccoon eyeing her from the ferns a few feet away. They were both still.

Samantha slowly placed her right hand over her heart and pressed gently. The raccoon sniffed the air briefly before trotting towards her. Circling Samantha once, she rose up on her hind legs and directed a small whirring call back to the ferns. Three waddling kits emerged, joining their mama at Samantha's feet. She guessed they must be a few months old; round and fuzzy, with velvety ears and huge dark eyes that blinked up at her. Their mother moved onward and they followed, glancing back at Samantha one at time before turning and sprinting into the shadows.

"Happy foraging," she whispered after them, smiling.

Stepping toward the giant beech tree, Sam ran her hands over the bark. It seemed to have muscle beneath, firm and rippled. The base of the tree was almost double the width of the trunk above her head. Walking around it once last year, she had counted fifteen steps, heel to toe.

There were dozens of roots, disappearing into the soil like strong animal legs. Bubbly moss covered the bark on one side of the trunk near the ground. From there she took five giant steps away from the tree. Dropping to her knees, she cleared away a small patch of the forest floor. Her fingers felt around in the crumbly soil, among rocks and twigs, searching. Finally, she found it: a thick vine, fashioned into a loop just the size of her fist.

She pulled at it gently, and stood to lift a moss-covered, hatched door. Then she propped it open with the thick rod that lay inside it. The opening was just big enough for her to fit through, and she carefully lowered herself down onto a wooden ladder built into the dirt wall below. Four steps down, she reached up to slide the rod away and the hatch thumped shut above her head. Dirt tumbled in after her, peppering her head and shoulders. She sputtered to keep it out of her mouth.

Climbing down steadily, she counted five steps before jumping down the final few and shaking off the rest of the dirt. She blinked a few times and rubbed some dust from her eyes as they adjusted to the light. It shone from her left, where a narrow, low corridor glowed in the corner. She could smell the burning fire that cast an orange and yellow light into the space under the hatchway.

"Samantha!" Walter's faint, deep voice welcomed her from the corridor. "Thank you for venturing out this evening to help us." His small, shadowed figure approached her. "Marta and Tom are finishing up with their packs and will be ready to join you shortly. Is it chilly tonight? Please come wait by the fire!" He motioned for her to join him and turned to head back into the corridor.

"It's warmer than last week," Sam replied to Walter's question, crawling on all fours to follow him through the narrow passageway. "I didn't need my sweatshirt."

Once inside the next room, she could stand with ease. She loved the Great Hall with its timbered, curved walls and stone fireplace. Directly below the beech tree, the ceiling of the room grazed the top of her head. Roots tangled among the beams. An oak staircase wound up the wall, leading to a doorway under the roots of the tree. A dozen little tables with benches filled the center of the room. Beautiful woven tapestries depicting the woods in different seasons decorated the walls.

"The wind is howling, isn't it?" Walter noticed. Samantha sat down cross-legged next to him and nodded. They both listened to the whistling and whirring noises above them.

Samantha adored Walter. Even though he was only as big as her father's hand, he was very strong and sturdy. He was always glad to see her. His bright eyes were the color of jade. Over the three years Samantha had known him, his dark brown hair had turned gray. Still, he looked much like the grandparents everyone knew, only much smaller.

Marta and Tom appeared from the double doors at the end of the Great Hall, carrying packs and gear. They wore sweaters made of soft, brown felt. Their packs were fashioned out of the same fabric. They each lugged a rolled up sleeping bag and mat, as well as a basket that Samantha assumed was filled with a few days' supply of food and water. They seemed about to drop all these things because of the weight, so Samantha got up to assist them. Greeting her warmly, they accepted her help.

Marta handed up her pack. "Just what we needed, a pair of big hands!"

"Sam, thank you for being here. We really appreciate it," added Tom. They both smiled warmly at her.

Tonight's job was simple enough. Marta and Tom were traveling to the Morley's house for a training session with the twins. They needed Samantha to help get them there safely. If they made the journey without her it would take many hours and would be very dangerous.

Samantha had thought long and hard to come up with a solution for the best way to make these trips. She had constructed different carriers for them to ride in a special pack on her back. However, Marta tended to get motion sickness when they tried this. Samantha understood. She got carsick on long, bumpy rides with her family in their minivan.

So, Marta and Tom would hike the whole way. Samantha would gently lift them over large rocks or logs in their path. Even so, the trek was hard for their small legs, with so much climbing. On her own Samantha could cover that distance in less than twenty minutes, but for them it took over an hour. She found it easy to be patient with them. It wasn't so easy with her little brother at home.

"All set?" Walter inquired, taking Marta's basket and handing it up to Samantha. She placed it inside her own backpack, along with Tom's pack and the rest of their gear. Marta smiled up at her, and then gave her father a farewell hug.

Walter returned the hug and gave Tom a set of hardy pats on the back. "Be safe out there!"

"We are in good hands with Samantha's guidance and care," Tom assured him.

"If you have everything, we should get going," Sam whispered. She had learned the hard way that her normal speaking voice was too loud for the Woodlanders' tiny ears. "The wind might slow us down a bit tonight. There are bound to be some branches down along the way."

The four of them nodded to one another and turned to head down the narrow corridor. Samantha went first on hands and knees, pushing her backpack in front of her.

Standing in the next chamber, Sam stretched

her arms and legs as best she could in the small space. She carefully picked up Tom and placed him near the top of a tiny ladder built into the dirt wall. Then, she lifted Marta to a spot a few steps below him, and they climbed the rest of the way up on their own. Sam put on her backpack, started up the big ladder and joined them at the top.

They couldn't manage the hatched doorway without her help. Usually, when the Woodlanders came and went from the homestead alone, they used the staircase in the Great Hall. It led up to a double door, about seven inches tall and eight inches wide. From outside, Samantha couldn't see it unless she got down low on the ground, as it was deep inside the roots. Sometimes one of her winter tasks was clearing away the snow and ice from the doorway after a storm.

Samantha knew of three other entrances to the homestead, located in different sections of the woods. Each was hidden in the roots of old trees. This hatch was the only place large enough for a Protectling, and it was used on a night like this when supplies were carried.

After Samantha helped Tom and Marta out of the hatchway, she spent a few moments closing and covering the door. She spread dirt over it, careful to cover the ring deeply. Standing up, she kicked bunches of pine needles and moss over it for good measure. When she was satisfied, she turned to see

Tom and Marta waiting patiently, sitting on a smooth rock.

Tom stood and reached for Marta's hand as he looked up through the branches. "That moon is delightfully bright!"

"Perfect night for a hike," smiled Marta, as the three of them set off towards the trail.

"I saw a mother raccoon with three little ones earlier, right there," Sam pointed. She was eager to let them know that their suggestion for peaceful animal encounters had worked beautifully.

Tom nodded. "It works every time. They don't have our language, but they can sense your intention if you concentrate on what you are feeling in your heart. The mother raccoon knew not to be afraid of you when you were focusing on your affection for her."

Tom told a colorful story about an encounter with a fisher cat a few years ago. "Kind of like a cross between a badger and cat, but with really sharp teeth!" The hand-on-the-heart gesture had worked then, but he wasn't eager to see if it would work again.

Marta agreed. "That was terrifying! I think we can assume he wasn't hungry, or it wouldn't have mattered how adored he felt."

They all laughed at this, although it wasn't funny to think about the dangers the Woodlanders faced in the forest. Foxes, fisher cats, red-tailed hawks, owls, the occasional dog on the trail ... Samantha knew the greatest danger of all was not a furry or feathered one, but her own kind. She stopped laughing at this certainty: her greatest challenge was to prevent that encounter from ever happening at all.

After seeing Tom and Marta safely to the Morley's, Samantha walked through the neighbors' back yard to her house. She quietly climbed the braided ladder, and pulled it up after her. Stepping inside, she rolled it up carefully and tucked it under her mattress.

Next to the green glow of her nightlight, she could see that her clothes were muddy, so she stuffed them into the bottom of the hamper. She changed into her favorite pajamas, printed with rows of perfectly sharpened colored pencils.

She climbed onto her bed, snapped on the lamp, and reached into her nightstand for her red-covered sketchbook and pencils. Its pages were almost full. She would need a new one soon. Finding a blank page near the end, she drew a fat raccoon, and three little ones with big eyes, surrounded by ferns. Her eyelids grew heavy, and she fell asleep with the light on, pencil in hand.

MAY

Marta felt weary after camping out at the Morley's for several nights. She longed for her own bed back at the homestead. Tom had set up a comfortable space for them in the linen closet behind the winter bedding that had been stored for the season. They tried to sleep there during the day. The babies' two naps and most of the night were for training. Marta and Tom split the Dreamguiding sessions in the middle of the night. A fair amount of climbing and hiding made for tiring work.

From their cozy spot behind the blankets in the closet, Marta could hear Beth and Paul finishing up bath time with the twins down the hall. Tom was next to Marta, patiently mending his pack with needle and thread in near darkness. They heard Beth's voice over the giggling and splashing.

"Paul, can you bring me some clean towels, please?"

"Coming right up!" Paul flung open the linen closet and hastily grabbed at some towels. The blankets came tumbling down with them, exposing

Tom and Marta's hiding place.

Startled, Tom pricked his palm with the needle and winced silently in pain. The two of them sprawled face down on the shelf, barely able to conceal themselves behind the one blanket left. Marta's heart was pounding as she buried her face in her sleeping bag.

They were on the top shelf, so Paul didn't see them. He mumbled to himself as he stuffed blankets back up there, dangerously smothering Marta and Tom under heaps of bedding. The closet door slammed shut, accompanied by Paul's muttering.

Tom frantically dug out from under the disorder. He was desperate to create some breathing space for Marta. The two of them climbed out from under a quilt, gasping for air.

"Are you okay, Dear?" Tom panted, unable see her face in the darkness. She reached over and held his hands in hers. Their panic slowly faded.

"I'm fine now, but we can't stay here. They will want to tidy up this mess. We still have two more days of training left. Let's pack up our things and set up somewhere else." They both knew this was necessary.

"While you're starting tonight's Dreamguiding session, I'll find us a new spot," Tom promised. They quickly rolled up their sleeping bags and filled the packs and basket.

Climbing down the shelves with all their things

was tough. Paul and Beth were still tending to the twins in the bathroom, so Marta and Tom struggled to push open the door and scampered down the hall to the twins' room. They knew they could hide out on the windowsill for a bit until bedtime.

After climbing up the crib with their packs and sleeping bags, Marta was spent. Sweat was running down Tom's face. They looked at each other with sympathy and collapsed on the sill.

"I hope I don't fall asleep during training tonight," Marta gasped.

Tom rubbed her shoulders. "You'll do fine. Don't worry."

Beth and Paul came into the room carrying the babies. The twins were babbling happily, ready for bed.

Paul laid the babies down, side by side. "Next month we should get another crib, so they can get used to sleeping apart."

"They are getting too big to share this one," answered Beth. She reached over and pulled the curtains closed, almost knocking Tom off the sill. Marta patted his arm gently to calm his nerves. They listened to Beth and Paul leave the room and close the door behind them.

The twins were sleepy after their bath and dozed off right away. Marta was grateful. She wasn't sure she could tolerate any baby tears after the stressful evening in the linen closet. As Tom set off to explore new camping options in the house, she worried about him. She dismissed her fears because he was a clever and capable man. It was time for Dreamguiding, which would require all of her energy.

She took a few deep breaths and set to work, climbing down from the sill and into the crib. The babies were lying on their bellies, snoring softly. Crawling carefully between them, she moved Oliver's right hand to Paige's left, linking them. Then she placed her own hands on top of their pudgy fists. Marta smiled.

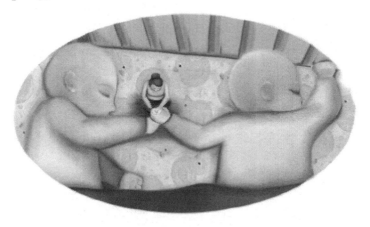

Where had Tom said he left off in the story? Oh yes, Walter's birth. It was in summertime. Marta closed her eyes and focused on creating some images in her mind. As long as she kept her hands on them, Marta's thoughts could flow into their dreams. After this bond was cemented in a few years, she would be able to communicate with them from far away, simply by focusing her thoughts.

Now, if she could pace her breathing to match theirs, the images in her mind would fill their dreams. It required intense concentration, but Marta could do it for hours after all these years of Dreamguiding.

Taking a deep breath, she closed her eyes and imagined herself standing in front of the giant beech tree, admiring its smooth bark and strong trunk. Grassy fragrances of a sunny morning surrounded her. Picturing herself walking around the large tree, she found the double door hidden within its roots and reached for the handle. Opening it, she descended the large winding staircase into the Great Hall.

In her imagination, she saw the room filled with several generations of happy Woodlanders. They were celebrating. A proud father and mother were presenting their baby boy to the admiring crowd. There was a tall cake on a table, surrounded by handmade gifts. A guitar player strummed a beautiful, quiet melody. The father cleared his throat and announced proudly: "His name is Walter Evergreen." The baby blinked large jade eyes, and yawned sleepily.

Marta could only imagine what her father looked like as a baby, of course. This part was a bit of fun for her. Dreamguiding could be very dangerous in the wrong hands for this reason. The Dreamguider could create any story, without regard for the truth. In their training with Walter's father, Henry, Marta and Tom had taken oaths to be honest and truthful at every turn. The Master Dreamguider was bound to honor the truth, as well as the freedom and will of others. The process was never to be used toward ill or evil, nor personal gain of any kind. Dreamguiding was only used to teach Protectlings everything they would need to know to be the guardians the Woodlanders needed.

Marta knew that once a Protectling reached a certain age, selfish thoughts and ideas began to emerge in earnest. Sometimes, a kid grew up to become a selfish adult. The development of greed was common. Marta knew the history well. For this reason, all Protectlings were children, without exception.

Opening her eyes and placing her hands in her lap, Marta's thoughts turned to Samantha. With a slow smile she recalled sitting like this in Sam's crib years ago, the infant's warm hand around her own. Samantha would be turning twelve soon. Feelings of affection and gratitude for the girl soured into deep sadness. Samantha's final days as a Protectling would be upon them soon.

In the next room, Tom felt a sudden, small ache in his chest. He wondered if everything was going well with Marta's work. He paused to focus his thoughts on her lovely face and capable hands, her devotion to whatever was in front of her. This soothed him. He hoped the warm feelings would reach her own heart as well.

With renewed energy, Tom looked around the cluttered room. Paul and Beth had littered it with a mess of objects and boxes from setting up the nursery. They wouldn't be cleaning it up anytime soon. A minute ago the space had left him feeling overwhelmed and tired. Now he saw that it provided perfect spaces for their hidden camp.

Under the window stood a desk that Paul had removed from the nursery to make room for the crib. It was covered with catalogs and magazines. An old wing-backed chair sat in the corner. Some curtains were folded upon it.

He climbed a front chair leg and pulled himself onto the cushion. Getting behind the pile of curtains, he pushed the top layer over the edge. He watched half the fabric tumble over and puddle on the carpet.

He jumped down and slid along the silky fabric with a swish, landing in a heap. With half the curtain still on the cushion above, a hidden room was created beneath the chair. He pulled at the cloth, working for few minutes to further hide the space before walking over to the door. From there he inspected his design, deciding that it looked acceptably messy. Smiling with satisfaction, he set to work constructing a snug, welcoming shelter for Marta's rest.

★　★　★

Several days after dropping off Marta and Tom at the Morley's, Samantha returned there in the middle of the night. There was no moonlight to guide her, and using a flashlight was not an option. She stayed off the sidewalk and crept close to the houses. Tonight she would be escorting Tom and Marta back to the homestead after their four-day training session with Oliver and Paige. The Woodlanders were clever in their efforts to stay out of sight. Samantha was amazed by their bravery in the face of constant hazards. She looked forward to hearing stories from them both.

The air was just warm enough. Sam had chosen a dark blue fleece and jeans to blend in with the black night. Spring peepers chirped from a nearby pond, keeping time with her tiptoeing steps. The plan was to meet Tom and Marta in the backyard by the kitchen door. The neighbors had a cat, so timing was very important. Marta and Tom could not hang around waiting alone for even a few moments.

Rounding the back of the house, Sam approached the meeting place. She was a few minutes early, so she sat down in the grass. It sounded like a thousand insects were talking to each other all around her. A couple of bats swooped around in messy loops over the yard.

From the house, she heard a noise at the kitchen window. Sam rushed over to give them a hand opening it. Their tiny faces lit up when they saw her. Tom was relieved to tuck his rope into their pack and let Samantha lift them off the sill. They felt like delicate birds in her hands. One at a time, she placed them carefully onto the grass before reaching in to grab the rest of their belongings and closing the window.

It was best not to talk until they were safely out of the yard and into the woods. The spring grass was just beginning to come in, so they made quick time through it. Samantha stepped alongside them carefully. In the darkness, she could barely see their outlines and counted on their movements to keep track of them. She wished she could carry them, but they always preferred to walk.

Finally, they reached the trail into the forest. Two large hemlocks marked its pine needle path.

Tom climbed onto a log and looked up at Sam. "I think it would be wise to light a lantern. What do you think, Samantha?"

Sam was relieved by this suggestion, as the woods seemed even darker than the yard.

"Great idea," she whispered. A tiny glass lamp was retrieved from their pack. Marta dug around in the basket for a jar of butternut oil, and filled the base of the lantern. Tom struck a pin-sized match and lit the wick. Their faces appeared in its glow, flickering golden yellow. The light wasn't much brighter than a firefly, but it would help Sam keep them in her sights. She was grateful for it. Tom held it out in front of them, illuminating the trail.

"How did the training go?" she asked her little companions. They trekked along, sharing tales of their adventurous days and nights in the Morley house. Oliver and Paige were growing and changing each day. It was obvious to Sam that Marta and Tom were smitten with the twins. She wondered if her own training had been like this.

"Paul and Beth are wonderful parents," Marta commented.

Tom agreed. "They are kind and gentle, and sing to the babies often, more than most Dumans."

Samantha had heard this term before among the Woodlanders, but thought it was just a mistake.

"Do you mean 'humans'?" she questioned him.

Tom and Marta exchanged a glance, and he took a deep breath before answering.

"No. They are humans, just like we are, but we call all the people who live in your society 'Dumans'. It is an old term, referring to their nature. It is so different from our own." He stepped carefully around a pinecone.

Sam frowned. "What do you mean, their

nature?"

Tom answered slowly. "A person's nature is what comes naturally to them—how they act and think and feel. It is in our nature to be curious. We share that with Dumans. Other characteristics, we do not share." Tom shifted the lantern to his other hand.

"Like what?" Sam asked. She listened to their footsteps treading on the soft pine needles. After a long pause, Tom seemed to pick up the pace a bit.

"Somewhere along the way, their character shifted from human beings to human doings. So we call them Dumans," Tom told her. "I hope you are not offended by this, Samantha. We don't mean it to be negative in any way. It is simply a name that came about as a description. We have great respect for the Dumans." Marta and he nodded at one another, and looked down at their feet as they walked.

Samantha was quiet for a moment. She did feel a bit offended. Although it rhymed with 'human', the word sounded unfavorable to her. She didn't want to be different from the Woodlanders in something as important as character. Her steps began to feel heavy.

"Am I a Duman?" Sam asked them. She tried to hide the despair in her voice.

"You are a Protectling," Marta answered. "You know things most Dumans have forgotten." She turned away from the lantern.

"Dumans live differently than we do, but we also have a lot in common," added Tom, his eyes looking upward to follow Sam's face. This didn't comfort Samantha.

"Why can't my mom and dad be Protectlings?" she wondered aloud. "They're both really kind, and they always help people, and ..."

She couldn't think of something else to add. It seemed obvious to her all at once that they would not be able to do her job as a Protectling, for many reasons. Unanswered questions popped up, one after another, into her mind, confusing her further. It seemed to get darker in the woods around them.

"I think you understand why they can't be Protectlings, Sam." Marta looked up at her. "Dumans are too busy to look after tiny people in the woods. Unless there would be something for them to gain from it, they might not do it," she explained. "This is also the reason we must remain hidden from them."

"There was a time in the past when some Dumans wanted to capture us and keep us in cages for their entertainment," Tom added. "That is our greatest fear, worse than any threat from wild animals." Tom and Marta both shuddered, recalling stories told by Walter and his father, Henry.

Sam knew this history. It was clear to her, although it didn't calm her mind to understand it.

Instead, a dawning puzzle began to bother her. It made her uneasy, so she shook her head and concentrated on the lantern bobbing in Tom's hand. She focused on the tiny flame as it danced.

"Speaking of wild animals, we should pick up the pace," Tom encouraged them. "I bet the night creatures are all out hunting." He laughed nervously.

A screech owl replied from a nearby tree, prompting them to move on. Sam was determined to get them safely to the beech tree, so she took a deep breath and lifted her chin as she walked.

Even in the pitch darkness, the woods were alert with a melody of croaks, buzzes and peeps. Each step Sam took silenced the area ahead of them, so that the unseen critters seemed to remain in the distance. She enjoyed identifying them: toads, owls, crickets, frogs ... It was a game she played to distract her troubled mind. The three of them plodded on without speaking.

Up ahead a large granite boulder marked the spot where they would head off the trail into the thicket that surrounded the beech tree. This time of year it was dense with saplings and prickly currant bushes.

Sam went first to create a path for Marta and Tom. It was slow going. The three of them crept carefully along, sticking close together.

Samantha was still thinking about their earlier

conversation. As they emerged from the brambles into the clearing around the huge beech tree, she decided to ask one more question.

"Marta, you said that I know things the Dumans have forgotten?" Sam inquired. "What things?"

They headed in the direction of the hatchway and were almost upon it before Marta answered.

"Most Dumans have forgotten how to be happy, Samantha," she revealed, taking off her pack and sitting upon it. Tom placed the lantern at Marta's feet and sat next to her, while Sam felt around in the dirt for the handle to the doorway.

"Not all of them, of course," Marta added. "Your family is happy. They work hard to be useful and to serve others. But Duman society is polluted by selfishness and greed, and striving for power." Marta faced Sam, and continued. "That only leads to misery and suffering."

Samantha dug around for the hatchway, listening intently. She lifted it, and propped it open for them. She wouldn't need to go in with them. They were safely home.

"Think about what makes you happiest, Samantha." Marta looked at her with raised brows. Sam helped them onto the ladder below, thinking, but it only took a moment for her to answer.

"That's easy—helping the Woodlanders makes me most happy." There were other fun things, like

Creepy Tag, drawing, or being with her family, but the feeling she got from being a Protectling was far above any of these. It was important work, and she felt good doing it. Even when it was hard and uncomfortable it was delightful.

Marta smiled from her foothold. "You will always know how to be happy, Sam. It is as simple as that."

The three of them said goodnight, although it was really closer to morning. Sam watched them climb down before closing the hatchway and covering it with care. She felt content in a job well done. As she stood to head home, tiredness overshadowed any other thoughts, and she looked forward to her bed.

JUNE

Samantha awoke on a sunny Saturday morning to the smell of waffles. The sweet, buttery fragrance was enough to rouse her out from under the covers. She was drowsy still, having spent several hours in the dark getting Marta and Tom to the Morley's for another training session with the twins.

As she sat up, threw back the blankets, and planted her feet on the floor, an uneasy feeling tingled in her belly. Something was not as it should be. Her cloudy, sleepy brain was having trouble waking up.

"Why did you sleep in your clothes?" Jared asked from the doorway. "Why do you have twigs in your hair? Your face is dirty." He was clutching his stuffed bunny, regarding her with interest.

Her eyes opened wide and darted down to take in her jeans and tee shirt. Her heart raced after his questions. He always asked so many. She reached up to feel the brambles tangled in her hair.

Samantha was fully awake now. Panic halted her breathing as her brother impatiently turned away and headed down the stairs to find some answers.

"Jared, wait! Come back!" Sam called. Desperately, she thought of a way to stop him.

"I have a story to tell you!" She yelled in his direction. This brought him racing into her room, bounding onto her bed. Stories were his favorite thing.

He looked down at her covers. "There's grass in your bed, and dirt. You're going to be in trouble," he added with concern.

Samantha felt a deep affection for him. She was grateful that it was Jared who saw her first this morning, and not her mom or dad. She'd be able distract him from the evidence of her night in the woods. Her parents would not have been so easily fooled.

How could she have been so careless? She was always thoughtful and thorough. Never had she fallen asleep before setting everything in order. She barely remembered climbing back in through the window at two in the morning. She had been so tired.

Looking toward the window, she held her breath. She reached down slowly to feel under her mattress. There she found the soft, strong braids of her ladder tucked away. She collapsed back against her pillow in a heap of relief. Jared was watching her, waiting.

"Tell me the story, Sammy. Finish the one from before about the rockets." Jared seemed to have forgotten about the dirt and grass.

Gratefully, Samantha launched into a colorful tale about Jared the astronaut and his first mate, Bunny. Her brother tenderly pulled the twigs from her hair as he listened to the story. The explorers were speeding through space about to land on Mars when their dad stopped in the doorway. Samantha carefully pulled the covers around them.

"Waffles are ready," her dad announced with a smile before heading down the stairs.

"Two more minutes!" Jared yelled hoarsely after him. He begged Sam to land the rocket so they could get to breakfast. She did so, then grabbed her robe and wiped her face clean with the hem of her sleeve. Jared stood up on the bed and then leapt for the door. Sam followed him, satisfied with a quick glimpse in the mirror.

"Are there chocolate chips in my waffle?" Jared asked, as he jumped into his chair, landing on his knees.

"Not today, Buddy. We're all out," his dad replied. "How was the trip, Sam?" he said, turning his attention to his daughter.

She froze. "What trip?" Her voice came out in a bizarre chirp, causing a burst of laughter from Jared.

"You sound like a bird!" Her brother giggled.

While he and his dad cracked up, she stuffed a large bite of waffle into her mouth. In her distress, it tasted bitter.

"The trip to the moon, silly," her dad explained. Jared was quick to give some details.

"Sam didn't go to the moon, just me and Bunny." He looked down at his furry friend tucked under his arm. Pointing his fork at Sam, he informed Bunny that his sister needed a bath.

Her father regarded her with raised eyebrows. She responded with a shrug and stuffed her mouth full again.

Their mom sat down with her coffee mug. "Nice try, Jared. You're the one with syrup all over your face." She smiled, tossing a napkin at him. Jared focused all his attention on avoiding the tub, wiping his mouth in earnest. Sam relaxed, and took another bite. This one was sweet and buttery.

After breakfast, Samantha returned to her room. She carefully cleaned up the bed and tossed an alarming amount of twigs out the window. Uneasiness hung over her as she knelt to rub a muddy footprint from the rug. This could not happen again. She made a silent promise to be more careful next time.

Next week, there would be another nighttime trek to the Morley's. The Woodlanders spaced these out to make sure Sam got caught up on her rest. She was always excited to receive their instructions, which arrived in her dreams. She would wake up knowing a time and place to meet them. If she couldn't be there, she would let them know by simply thinking about a message for them before falling asleep at night. This required planning, but it seemed to work just fine. She smiled to herself, looking forward to their company. Helping them in their work pleased her more than getting presents or drawing.

★ ★ ★

The last week of school presented the summer's first really hot day. Sam was wearing shorts, as the forecast predicted eighty degrees. The morning was still cool, so she shivered at the breakfast table. Her mother came over and sat next to her.

"I have a surprise for you, Sam," she announced, waving a folded piece of paper clasped between her fingertips. "I think you're going to be really exited!" She pushed the sheet over toward Sam's cereal bowl with a big smile.

"Open it!" yelled Jared. He bounced around in his chair, sloshing milk onto the table.

Sam reached over and unfolded the paper. In large brown letters shaped liked logs, the words 'CAMP WALDEN' were surrounded by leaves and ladybugs. A canoe with crossed oars floated at the bottom of the page. In the middle it said:

Dear Samantha,

We are looking forward to meeting you! Your session begins June 30th. Here is a list of the things you will need to bring: ...

The checklist blurred before her eyes as Sam faked a smile. "Wow, this looks great, Mom. Thanks," she mumbled.

Jared stopped chewing his cereal. "You don't seem excited. Not one bit."

Her mom looked confused. "I thought you would jump up and down over this! You love the woods so much. Don't you think sleeping in a cabin out there will be fabulous?"

Samantha searched for something to say but just sat there staring at the paper. She didn't have any way to tell her mother that the woods in New Hampshire were too far away from the Woodlanders.

"Well, maybe you'll get more excited after we shop for that packing list," announced her mom after Samantha's silence. "We can get started today after school." She grabbed the list from Sam and put on her reading glasses to study it.

Sam wanted to stop this before it went any further. "Mom, I really would rather stay home all summer if that's okay—" She tried to sound casual but it seemed to backfire.

"Nonsense," answered her mother. "This is such a treat, and we already paid for it so you'd better say 'Thank You' and turn around that frown of yours." She rolled up the sheet of paper and gently rapped Sam on the nose with it. It was clear there would be no pleading.

★　★　★

Saturday afternoon was warm and sunny. Samantha walked down the street and turned onto Snapdragon Circle. Palmer's house was number sixteen. His mother was in the front yard, kneeling in the flowerbed. She wore a pink sun hat and green gloves, and was digging along the path to the front door. Every June she planted pink and white impatiens there. By the middle of July they exploded into a trail of color that Sam loved to follow.

"Hi Mrs. Batista," Sam waved from the sidewalk.

"Oh, hi there, Samantha. How are you?" She took off her gloves and stood up to greet her. There was a smudge of dirt on her upper lip that looked like a mustache. Sam tried not to laugh.

"I'm good, thanks. I just came over to say goodbye to Palmer. I'm leaving for camp tomorrow." They both smiled and then frowned.

"We'll miss you," Palmer's mom said gloomily.

"He's in the backyard, in the treehouse, I think. Will you go through the kitchen and grab him an apple or something, please? He hasn't had lunch yet."

Sam nodded, and Palmer's mom thanked her as she put her gloves back on, adding another smudge to her forehead.

Sam opened the side door and stepped into the kitchen, which was one of her favorite places. It always smelled really good, like pizza and cookies. There was a bowl of fruit on the counter. She grabbed a banana and a green apple and headed out the sliding doors into the backyard.

In the corner near the woods stood the treehouse. It was really more of a fort, built on stilts and not up in a tree, but it was amazing. Palmer's older brothers and his dad had built it. It looked like a ship of some kind, with a pointed front deck. There was a ladder up the side and double glass doors from a real house as an entrance. It made the single room inside warm and sunny. Also, there was a zip-line from a platform in the back into the woods. That was the best part.

Sam walked toward it and stopped at the foot of the ladder.

"Hey, anyone up there?" she hollered. "I brought you a snack." There was no reply. She waited a few moments, studying a bruise on the banana. Finally, the door opened and Palmer leaned out with a bored look on his face. Sam held up the fruit.

"Come on up." Palmer's head withdrew, and she approached the ladder. There was a basket on the ground under the treehouse with a rope attached. She placed the fruit inside it, along with a packet of gummy worms from her pocket. Then she yanked on the rope and Palmer pulled it up through a hole in the floorboards while Sam climbed the ladder.

She saw him sitting cross-legged inside, examining the contents of the basket. He was obviously in a bad mood. He didn't look at her. Instead, he focused all his attention on the choice before him: apple, banana or gummy worms.

Stepping into the little room, Sam rubbed at a

knot in the wood of the floorboards with the toe of her sneaker. It was unlike Palmer to ignore her. She wondered if maybe he was mad at her.

"I thought you were coming over for lunch so that we could hang out before I leave for camp tomorrow," she said.

Palmer picked up the apple and rubbed it on his shirt. Sam thought this added some dirt to it instead of cleaning it. He took a big bite and looked past her out the door. She sat down and crossed her legs.

"I forgot, sorry." He chewed noisily, and took another bite before swallowing the one in his mouth.

Sam sighed. "My mom made your favorite strawberry and hazelnut spread sandwiches. I ate yours," she added, starting to feel annoyed.

He looked straight at her then, and swallowed hard. He reached into the basket and took out the pack of gummy worms, tearing it open. He picked through them to find a yellow one, and handed it to her.

The yellow ones were her favorite. She accepted the gesture with relief.

He took another bite of his apple. "I'm sorry," he said. "I didn't really forget. I just wanted to hang out here by myself. It will go by really fast, two weeks. I have baseball camp at the town center every day, so I'll hardly miss you at all." He spit an apple seed onto the floor.

Sam nodded and ate the gummy worms, ignoring his bad manners. She could tell that Palmer was mad that she was going away to camp.

"Right. It'll go by fast," she agreed. Long moments of silence hung between them. Sam reached over and pressed her thumb into the banana, creating another bruise.

"Anyhow, Mom and Dad said you could come with us to drop me off at camp if you want. It's an hour drive so maybe that wouldn't be fun, but whatever. We're leaving around 10." Sam hoped he would want to come along.

Palmer stood up and faced into the woods. He threw the rest of the apple hard out the back window, and they both listened to it smash against a nearby tree.

Sam sighed and flicked the apple seed off the floor in his direction. "Have a great time at baseball camp." She stood up and headed out to descend the ladder. She stopped halfway down, adding softly, "I'll hardly miss you at all either, Palmer." She jumped the rest of the way down and headed home.

Palmer knelt down and picked up the half empty gummy worm packet. He folded over the top before placing it carefully in his pocket.

★ ★ ★

The next morning, Samantha had a sunrise meeting with Marta and Tom at the beech tree and didn't want to be late. Her parents would be up early, eager to pack the car and get on the road. She left a note on her bed so they wouldn't worry if they went in to wake her up and found her gone:

Out for a morning walk,
saying goodbye to the woods

Back for breakfast – waffles,
please!

XXOO, Sam

The dawn was dim all around her. Morning light ramped up with each step she took as she made her way into the woods. By the time she got to the beech tree, the pink and orange glow of the sky had warmed to pale yellow. Soft breezes rustled the leaves above, and the birds crooned from every direction. It sounded like she was in a tropical rainforest.

Marta and Tom were standing within the safety of the great tree's roots. Sam could see them peeking out from the shadows, watching for her. Their eyes met hers, and they waved happily, coming out into the light. They blended perfectly with the colors of the woods in their chocolate brown linen shirts and trousers. Marta wore a pine green fuzzy sweater, and Tom wore a cap made of the same fabric. On their feet were felt slippers, unlike the boots they wore for hiking.

"Good morning, Samantha," Marta waved up at her. Tom's arm was linked in hers as they stepped onto a large globe of moss. Sam sat down cross-legged in the pine needles next to them.

"Good morning," she responded. "Thanks for meeting with me so early. I wanted to say goodbye before I leave for camp. It's far away, and I won't be back for a few weeks. I wanted to make sure you didn't need anything." Marta and Tom shook their heads and assured her that they would be fine in her absence.

"I know it's a bad time for me to be away," Samantha added, as she picked at a patch of wild thyme growing next to the moss. She crushed a dozen tiny leaves between her thumb and forefinger and inhaled the woody scent.

Late June was when the Woodlanders took advantage of the low creek level to gather silt from its bottom. After digging it up, they spread it out on birch bark to dry in the sun before melting it in their kiln to make glass for lanterns and jars. It was a hard job that took many days and heavy hauling.

"Do not worry about the Mud Bake,

Samantha. There are plenty of hands to lighten the load," Tom promised her.

"You will be home in time for the Lantern Lighting, which is the best part anyhow," Marta added.

Samantha was happy to hear this. The celebrations and festivals the Woodlanders created to conclude their seasonal work were delightful— better than any holiday Sam could imagine. The Lantern Lighting was magical, and Sam was thrilled that they would include her even though she would miss out on all the hard labor.

"We will be excited to hear about the far away woods when you get back," Tom said eagerly. "It is not often we get the chance to hear tales from abroad. Perhaps you can carry a message for us to the Woodlanders there?"

Sam's eyes grew wide. "There are other Woodlanders?" She sat up taller, considering this possibility. It had never occurred to her before, but now seemed plain to see.

Marta and Tom nodded. "In any woods there are likely to be Woodlanders, although the average Duman won't see any signs of them," Marta explained.

"A Protectling will, if you look closely; wisps of smoke rising from tree tops mingling with the clouds, tiny footprints the size of almonds alongside streams, cattails missing their cottony tops ..."

"Different traces depending on the season," added Tom. "This time of year you might spot patches of moss missing where it has been collected for weaving felt, or trenches in the low creek beds after Mud Bake."

Samantha listened, imagining the scenes left behind by little gatherers.

"Perhaps you will meet other Protectlings as well," Tom told her. "Although you won't be able to tell just by looking at them. And of course no one would tell you—just as you would never speak of it. You will simply notice a warm connection within your heart."

Samantha was excited by the possibility. Suddenly the prospect of going off to camp no longer troubled her. She looked upon her small friends, knowing that she would miss them and her duties here, but eager for new adventures that awaited her in the woods of New Hampshire. She glanced at her watch and the brightening sky, ready to say goodbye.

"One more thing," Tom said, jumping down off his mossy perch and heading to the beech roots. He disappeared for a moment within, returning with a beechnut. It filled his small arms, but as he handed it up to Samantha, she accepted it between two fingers.

Turning it around in her hand, Sam studied the shape and feel of it. The outer plush husk had been removed, exposing a shiny, triangular shell. Soft and smooth, it was unlike the walnuts and pecans in the nut bowl at home. It had been opened, and sewn shut again with a leathery, purple twine.

"What's inside?" asked Sam, examining the fine line of stitching and perfect square knots at each end.

"A silk pouch filled with etched amber beads, along with a note of well wishes from all of us to all of them," Tom told her. "Also, Marta painted a map of our woods and a family tree naming everyone who lives among us. It is our custom to create such a gift whenever we have the chance to extend friendship outward to the greater family. It is called an amber token."

Samantha knew that some of the Woodlanders wore amber necklaces and bracelets made out of honey-colored beads, but she didn't know where they came from.

"What is amber?" she asked, admiring Marta's necklace. It glimmered in a ray of sunshine that beamed down on her from between the branches.

Marta reached up to feel the beads around her neck. "Sometimes when digging up dandelion roots we find pieces of amber," she explained. "It is tree sap that has hardened almost into a stone over many years. It doesn't look like much at first, but it polishes into the most beautiful color."

"Amber glows with the energy of the tree it

came from," Tom added. "Sometimes we find it at the bottom of the creek bed as well. Those pieces are especially old and precious."

Samantha looked down at the triangular nut-purse in her hand. She closed her fist over it.

"How am I meant to give it to them?" she asked.

"It is unlikely that you will see them," Tom answered. "Simply place it inside the roots of an old tree and it will be found eventually. They will recognize the purple twine as the sign of an amber token. It will be an exciting day for them to have word from afar," he smiled.

Sam felt hopeful. "Maybe I will see them." She stood and tucked the token into her pocket. Marta and Tom rose as well, brushing specks of moss spores from the seats of their pants.

"We will be thrilled to hear all about it when you return," Marta said as she jumped down from the mossy mound.

"Have a wonderful time while you are away, and we will see you soon," Tom added. They thanked her and turned toward the beech tree. Before ducking into the security of its roots, they waved to her, one hand raised, the other over their hearts. Samantha's worries about leaving the Woodlanders were erased.

Sam jogged back home, her pace quick and light. The sound of laughter from her yard drew her out of the woods. She looked up at the brightening sky over her house as she opened the gate. Ribbons of pink clouds were fading into a wide expanse the color of a robin's egg.

Closing her eyes, she inhaled the sweet scent of waffles. Across the yard, her family sat at the patio table, which was set for a special sendoff breakfast. They were sharing full plates with Lulu and Palmer, who both jumped up to greet her.

JULY

It was July 1965, and Walter Evergreen was looking forward to his eighth birthday. He and his father were planning an overnight camping trip at Woods Edge to celebrate. It would be a big adventure for Walter. The Woodlanders didn't travel far from the homestead often, without a Protectling. Walter and his father, Henry, made lists and gathered gear and supplies for the trip. It would take half a day to trek to the spot where the woods bordered the field by the old farmer's house. There was a stone wall there that would work well for a safe, overnight shelter. The boy's excitement grew each day as they consulted trail maps and prepared for the hike.

*   *   *

The farmhouse had seen better days. It needed a new coat of paint. The old barn next to it sagged a little here and there. Not far from the farmhouse, two men got out of a truck and walked toward the stone wall bordering the woods at the edge of the field. One of the men was tall and muscular. The buttons of his shirt strained over his large chest. The other man was short and thin, with a narrow face. They both paced around the edge of the woods, studying the land. The day was hot and dry.

"See, Martin? We can buy this land for practically nothing," the tall one said. He took off his cap and swept his arms open wide.

"Nothing goes for nothing, Jack." The short man turned around in a circle, admiring the landscape.

"I figure we can build thirty houses here, surrounding those woods over there." Jack waved his cap toward the dense trees several yards away.

Martin squinted. "Or, Jack, we could clear the woods and build sixty, make it a bigger development," he proposed.

Jack shook his head. "Not for sale, those woods. The farmer won't consider it. Says they're to be 'protected.'" His fingers made quote signs in the air. "He's setting up some sort of conservation plan in perpetuity." He shrugged.

"Perpa what?" Martin squinted again, confused. Jack put on his cap and stuffed his hands into the pockets of his shorts.

"I think it means forever, or a hundred years maybe. Whatever, we can't build there." Jack turned and started to walk back to the truck.

Martin didn't move. He was looking toward the

woods, working the numbers. *This housing development would make them lots of money, but they could make much more if they cleared the woods.*

"Offer him more cash," he shouted after Jack, running to catch up with him.

"I already tried that," Jack answered. "He's real stubborn. Has a soft spot for those woods—boyhood memories and all." He folded his arms over his big barrel chest and leaned against the truck. The noon sun was directly overhead, reflecting brightly on the windshield.

Martin was not ready to give up so easily. "Let's go talk to the old man." He pointed at Jack, wagging his finger with each word. "Everyone has a price."

They climbed into the blue Ford and slammed its dusty doors. The farmer, Mr. Rawlings, had let them borrow his truck to check out the acreage. The old Ford had over a hundred thousand miles on it, but was in good shape. Their shiny new Mustang would not have been able to handle the fields, so they had left it behind at the farmhouse. They saw it up ahead as they approached the gravel drive leading to the front porch. Jack drove slowly out of the bumpy meadow. Large grasshoppers crisscrossed in front of them.

Mr. Rawlings appeared on the porch with a pitcher of lemonade. Placing it next to three mason jars on a table, he shuffled over to one of the rockers and slowly lowered himself into it.

"Hello, boys!" He hollered in their direction, waving a crooked hand. Jack and Martin got out of the truck and joined him in the shade of the porch.

"Help yourselves to some delicious lemonade." He poured them each a glass. "Comes in a canister these days, you just add water! Can you imagine? Helen used to squeeze a dozen lemons and make simple syrup, took half an hour." The farmer shook his head in wonder. "She would be amazed! And, she would be sad to see the farm go, but it's time. I can't manage here alone anymore since she passed away. My daughter wants me to come live with her in Chicago." He took a few gulps from his glass.

Sitting down in one of the rockers, Martin sipped

his lemonade. It tasted weak and warm, but he finished it off and returned the glass to the rickety table.

"Delicious, thank you, Mr. Rawlings," he squinted at the old man and smiled. Jack was not able to pretend so easily. He made a face into his glass and placed it next to Martin's before sitting down in the third rocker.

"Please, boys. Call me Norm. It's short for Normal." The farmer looked seriously at each of them for a second before slapping his knee and hooting loudly with laughter. Jack joined him, clearly amused by the joke. Martin thought it was dumb. He knew the old man's name was Norman. He forced a chuckle. He crossed his legs and settled back into the rocker.

"Norm, we're very sorry for the loss of your dear Helen." He tilted his head and leaned forward. "I'm sure you miss her very much. I sense she is looking down on you right now from heaven."

Martin smiled then, looking up at the peeling blue paint on the porch ceiling. Norman and Jack followed his gaze with confusion. Jack shifted uncomfortably and began rocking noisily in his chair. Martin glared at him before continuing.

"Jack and I are both eager to make sure you have the security you deserve. I think that would mean doubling our offer, if you include the woods in the sale, along with the cleared land. Double the land, double the money," he concluded, opening his hands wide and then clapping them together loudly.

Norm frowned, startled by the noise. "I already told your friend here that the woods ain't for sale." He looked over at Jack, but was disappointed to see him picking at his fingernails.

"My grandfather and his brothers cleared this land," Norman told them. "Those stone walls were built one rock at time, dug up with their hands to create the fields for planting. Hundreds of trees felled, and the wood used to build this house, and the barn."

He turned his head to take in the faded red stain on the old barn. "He worked for decades to build this farm and take care of the land. So, you can understand how difficult it is for me to sell it to a couple of developers who plan to tear down my house and put in one of those newfangled culs-de-sac. What the heck does that word mean anyhow? It's ridiculous." He shook his head.

Jack spoke up. "It's a dead end street with a turn-around, great for kids to ride their bikes and play street ball—"

Martin cut him off with a scowl and interrupted. "Of course, we know how hard it is to sell your farm, Norm. But consider what a great family neighborhood this will become! We're going to call it 'Rawlings Meadow.'" He spread his arms wide toward the field. "All the streets will be named after flowers, like Primrose Lane and Snapdragon Circle," he explained.

Norman looked tired. "That sounds sillier than cul-de-sac," he said, shaking his head. Jack snorted, and

Martin glared at him again.

Norm rocked slowly back and forth. "As hard as it is for me see this farm paved over with stupid flowery-named streets, I'm a forward thinking man. I know the time has come for a neighborhood to grow here. I'm okay with that."

He stopped rocking and leaned forward, resting his elbows on his knees and clasping his hands together.

"The woods are a different story," he told them. "No amount of money will convince me that it's time for those trees and creatures to be destroyed. I will never change my mind about that." He nodded once, and poured himself another glass of lemonade.

Martin abandoned his plan to appeal to Norman's greedy side. Apparently he didn't have one.

"Well, Norm, the town might disagree with you," Martin said, squaring his shoulders. "They may think it's a good idea to double the size of this development. More tax dollars coming in that way." His mouth formed a thin line. "Jack and I can persuade them to hand over the land for development, so it really doesn't matter if you change your mind or not." He nodded once, copying Norm.

This didn't bother the old man. He was enjoying the sweet, tangy lemonade on his tongue. Looking over at Jack, he felt sorry for the young guy. He was obviously troubled by Martin's rude behavior, but too weak to do anything about it. A feeble character in a muscular body. Things were often not as they appeared, he thought.

Norm stood up and straightened his back. It cracked and complained loudly, but he ignored it.

"Let's get on with this, boys. Draw up the paperwork for the sale of the farm, and I'll sign it right away. You will find that I have already filed the papers with the town protecting those three hundred acres of woods, and it cannot be reversed. It's already conservation land in perpetuity. Now there's a word I like." He winked at Jack, and headed inside, letting the screen door slam behind him.

Martin glared at Jack, who stared back at him blankly.

"Why do you keep giving me the hairy eyeball? I told you about the perpa-whatever thing already," Jack said, as they walked to their shiny green Mustang. Martin reached for the car door handle. It was hot from roasting in the sun and burned his hand. Scorching air rushed out of the front seat when he opened the door. They both stood for a moment, letting in some fresh air. Martin pointed at Jack, which was starting to get on Jack's nerves.

"I'm not going to let that sentimental old man cheat us out of such a big profit," Martin told him. "Who cares about some stupid trees and chipmunks? Not me, and not you," Martin pointed, getting into the car and cursing at the scalding leather.

Jack looked over toward the tall oaks and pines. He knew it would be a hassle to buy the woods from the town, but he knew Martin was right. Everyone had a price.

★ ★ ★

Samantha was enjoying herself at camp. The grounds were beautiful, on the edge of an old pine forest, with a small lake and cozy cabins. She shared one with three girls her age, and a counselor.

After one week, Sam was able to explore the woods a bit. She was never allowed to go anywhere alone, you had to take a buddy. It was annoying. A day hike in the woods with a counselor and several other campers was her only chance to look for signs of Woodlanders. She brought along the amber token from Marta and Tom, hidden in her pack with her lunch and water bottle.

The forest felt magical to Sam. Old pines towered high above her, shading many acres. A deep carpet of soft pine needles paved the trail. A stream trickled nearby, and the hikers headed toward it.

Up ahead, Sam spotted a good place to leave the amber token. It was a giant twin pine, with a trunk separating into two boles above Sam's head. At its roots, a small triangular gap about the size of her hand caught her eye. To her, it looked like the perfect homestead entrance, and she imagined busy

Woodlanders scurrying below.

She planned to wait until after lunch to sneak over and tuck the beechnut inside when no one was looking. She took out her water bottle and took a sip. Checking the amber token, she found it a little damp, so she dabbed it on her shorts and stuck it in her pocket. She walked toward the stream where the counselor was laying out a blanket for lunch.

Sam was disappointed that she didn't recognize any other Protectlings at Camp Walden. Her bunkmates were mostly nice, except for one girl named Maddie. She was loud, and laughed when people got hurt, like when Sam stubbed her toe on the porch steps. Sam mostly tried to avoid her.

Maddie approached her now, and pounced on her, knocking Sam's water bottle out of her hand.

"Slowpoke Sam,'" Maddie sang, kicking the water bottle as Sam reached for it. They both watched it sail through the air and tumble towards the roots of the twin pine. Sam looked over at Maddie, thrilled to have an excuse to leave the group and head over to that tree.

"Thanks, Maddie." Sam smiled, bounding off to retrieve her water bottle. The counselor called over to Maddie to leave Sam alone and come set up for lunch. Confused and defeated, Maddie made her way back to the group.

Sam took her time. She reached into her

pocket and felt the amber token. She skipped the rest of the way over to the twin pine. Her water bottle sat where it had landed, nestled in some moss right next to the gap in the roots.

Checking to make sure no one was watching, Sam knelt down and reached her hand into the opening. A space widened inside, and she felt around in the dirt. Her knuckles bumped up against something straight and hard several inches to the left. It was a wall.

Stretching her arm deeper into the hole, she was able to explore it further. Her fingertips found a tiny round bump, then another one right next to it on the solid surface. Between them was a groove. Knobs on a tiny door ...

"Your water bottle isn't in there, Slowpoke." Maddie stood by Sam's feet with her arms crossed. Carefully, Samantha withdrew her arm from the hole and turned around. She hadn't heard Maddie approaching, and wondered how long she'd been there.

"Right, just a bunch of spider's webs," Sam said, sitting back against the entrance. She wiped her hand on her shorts. They were a bit sticky. She hadn't noticed till now. "I really want to catch one of the hairy speckled spiders that live in these pine trees," Sam lied, reaching for her water bottle.

"That's gross," Maddie responded, shaking her head. "You're weird. They sent me over to get you for lunch, so hurry up." She kicked the bottle again, just as Sam reached for it. Maddie sprinted off to tell the others about Sam's love of hairy spiders.

As she watched the bottle roll to a stop near the path, Sam wondered if she should leave the amber token here after all. Since she wasn't sure she would get another chance, she took it out of her pocket. Rubbing its smooth surface and tiny purple stitches, she closed her eyes and made a wish for its discovery. She looked over and watched the campers as they busily set up for lunch. Then, she reached behind her back and felt inside the hole. Dropping the beechnut, she pushed it inside until it bumped against the little door. She thought she heard some small pattering sound below, like slippers on steps, but as she strained to listen, it disappeared.

★   ★   ★

Martin and Jack drove along the gravel road, leaving dust in their wake. The Purchase and Sale Agreement sat in a folder between them on the car seat, ready to be signed. Norm was expecting them. They could see him there on the porch, sitting next to a pitcher of lemonade, pink this time.

"Great," Martin whined. "We'll get to hear all about newfangled, colored drink mixes now. Isn't it amazing! What will they think of next?" he teased.

Jack looked straight ahead. He liked Norm, and it bothered him to hear Martin make fun of him. He felt a connection to Norm, one that he couldn't explain. Besides, he thought pink lemonade was neat.

Martin was frustrated after their meeting with the town conservation board. It was impossible to overturn the land deal Norman had made. He was giving half of his money from the sale of the farm to the conservation fund, ensuring its security for generations to come.

"I was thinking," Martin said softly as the Mustang rolled to a stop in front of the farmhouse. He returned Norman's wave, smiling. "If there was a fire, and the woods burned down, there wouldn't be anything to conserve, would there? The town would be eager to let us clean up the mess and build a beautiful neighborhood in its place."

Jack froze, gripping the steering wheel. He was afraid to look at Martin. Slowly, he glanced over to see him smiling, like he had just heard some good news.

Martin pointed at him. "It's very dry this time of year. That cigar could easily start a fire in the brush. It would spread quickly ..."

"What cigar?" Jack hissed. "I don't smoke," he said defensively.

Martin redirected his wagging finger at the porch, and waved again.

Norm raised his cigar in response, and took a puff. A circle of gray-blue smoke expanded in front of him, and he peeked around it to welcome them.

"Boys!" Norm yelled in greeting. "Got those papers ready?" He stood up shakily, dropping his cigar. It rolled across the sloping porch, bumping down the stairs into the dry grass.

Jack sprang from the car, ran over to it, and stomped it into a pulp.

"Careful, Norm!" Jack scolded, kicking the smashed brown blob into the gravel. "You'll burn the place down," he warned.

Martin followed Jack up the steps, whispering behind him.

"Well done! Now he'll blame himself when he hears about it." Martin reached up to pat him on the shoulder, but Jack dodged the gesture.

"Got any more of those cigars, Norm?" Martin asked as he poured three mason jars of lemonade. He offered the first one to Jack, who accepted it with downcast eyes. "We should celebrate," Martin said, handing another glass to Norm, and saluting him with his own pink drink. The three of them clinked glasses.

"Yes, let's get you boys some cigars, have a proper toast here!" Norm nodded, putting down his glass and retreating into the house.

They heard him banging around in the kitchen. Jack leaned over toward Martin, hoping to halt this bad idea before it went any further. He couldn't think of anything to say, so he just took a few gulps of his pink *lemonade.*

"Here we go," Norman announced, shuffling through the doorway with three fat cigars in his fist.

Martin smiled. He hated cigars, always choking and sputtering, then feeling sick to his stomach after a few puffs.

"Those look great, Norm. Matches?" Martin asked. Norm fished into the pocket of his overalls, handing over a well-worn book of matches from Sully's Seed Shop. Jack took them and struck one, offering the flame to each man as he puffed to light his cigar. Jack placed the papers and the matches on the table and pulled a pen out of his shirt pocket.

"To Rawlings Meadow," Martin bellowed, raising his cigar in the air. Norm copied him with a smile, taking the pen from Jack and signing his name with a flourish. Jack went next, then handed the pen over to Martin.

Before taking it, Martin put his cigar in his mouth and clenched it in a jumbo grin. With one hand he grabbed the pen and signed his name on the line. His other hand closed over the book of matches, sliding them out of sight and into his back pocket.

AUGUST

Sam woke up at midnight to the sound of cicadas buzzing. Since coming home from camp, she appreciated having a room to herself. Her bed was big and comfortable.

It was hot, and the air was heavy. She climbed out of bed and put on the denim shorts and pink tank top she had laid out on her desk.

Tonight was her favorite night of the summer. The Lamp Lighting festival the Woodlanders held this time of year was magical. After weeks of gathering silt from the creek beds, drying it in the sun, and then carrying it all underground in felt-lined baskets, they melted it down in a kiln.

In sweltering heat at the furnace, the glassblowers made as many grape-sized glass bubbles as they could. The cooled balls were then made into lanterns in the workshop. It was a long and difficult process. A night of swimming in the lamplit stream was reward for all their hard work. It was a cherished tradition.

Sam was grateful to be included, since she had

missed all the work while away at camp. She had a surprise for the Woodlanders, and was looking forward to sharing it with everyone. Putting the small bundle in her pocket, she climbed out the window and headed into the woods.

A bright, yellow moon in the August sky provided a surprising amount of light. Fireflies blinked on and off in the shadows. As she approached the beech tree, Sam could hear tiny voices. Dozens of Woodlanders were gathered around the base of the tree, and more were coming out of the little doorway hidden in its roots.

Palmer was there, watching over them. Sam joined him, kneeling down in the moss where he was talking to Walter. Marta and Tom waved to her, and their teenaged daughter, Tara, blew Sam a kiss. Seeing them all again made her smile from ear to ear.

"Good evening, Samantha!" Walter addressed her. "Welcome back! Thank you for joining us tonight. Now that you are here we can line up and head out. Palmer, why don't you lead the way to the stream and Sam can bring up the rear."

Walter and his wife, Elsa, gathered the Woodlanders into a few long rows. Palmer picked up the crates of lanterns and put them carefully in his backpack. Sam did the same with a few baskets of goldenrod cookies and some clay jugs of honeysuckle punch. She placed them into her backpack cushioned between stacks of little green felt towels. In her hands she carried some jars of butternut oil.

Their night parade buzzed with excitement. The Woodlanders whispered and laughed, skipping and jumping to keep up with Palmer. Samantha took small steps. She was careful to watch that no one fell behind.

Arriving at the stream, Palmer took off his shoes and unpacked the crates of lanterns. Samantha followed the last of the Woodlanders over to the water. She found a spot for the butternut oil and snacks, and stacked the towels neatly. Her sneakers joined the pile of tiny boots that was forming on a flat rock in the moonlight.

In the clearing next to the stream, Walter was organizing the barefooted families into a large circle. They all wore the same gray linen tank tops and shorts, grown ups and children alike.

After three summers of Lantern Lighting, Sam and Palmer knew what to do. She helped him line up the lanterns in the grass. Each Woodlander came over to choose one. Then they sat down in the circle and waited quietly for the others. Elsa and Walter went around the circle, filling the base of each lamp with butternut oil. Once each lantern was ready, the group stood up. Walter's gentle voice broke the silence.

"As we enjoy the last warm nights of summer,

let us take a moment to be grateful for what has been provided for us. The ancient silt and sand melted down into glass for these lanterns." He held up his own imperfect globe by its twine handle. Elsa stood next to him and held up a jar of butternut oil. It reflected the moonlight.

"The nuts of the white walnut tree, dropped for us to gather," she added. "Their oil burns bright to light our way." She bent down and placed the jar in the grass and then reached into her pocket to remove a narrow beeswax candle. She struck a tiny match and lit it. Then, she put its flame to the wick in Walter's lantern, and it glowed brightly. She passed the candle over to the next Woodlander, and it went around the circle until every lantern was shining.

Palmer crossed the stream and stood on the bank at the other side. Sam stepped through the shallow water to follow him. They sat down on a log at the edge, dangling their feet in the cool water. The Woodlander's circle of light flickered. It formed a ball of yellow radiance that seemed to breathe.

Sam was mesmerized. She imagined herself small enough to stand in the middle of it. The spell was heightened by the sound of all the Woodlanders tapping their tiny fingernails against the glass of their lanterns.

Sam looked over to see Palmer transfixed.

"It sounds like dozens of little bells ringing," he said in a whisper. "And the light is dancing to it," he added. Sam smiled at this perfect description.

The tinkling melody from across the stream stopped, and Elsa stepped into the center of the circle.

"Shine light into the darkness, and always light the way for others." She raised her lantern and the Woodlanders raised theirs in response. Then, they all turned toward the stream and cheered, running with their lanterns swinging. They put them down in a line along the water's edge. The light reflected into the black water, glittering like diamonds in a ribboned mirror.

Splashing and laughter filled the air. The stream was flowing, but its level was low this time of year. Palmer watched the Woodlanders sloshing around in the shallow water and had an idea.

"Will you help me move a few of these rocks?" he asked Sam.

They jumped into the water and walked a few paces downstream. Palmer took a large rock from the grass and placed it in the water. Sam stacked a few more next to it until a deep, wide pool began to form in front of the rocks. They added two more large ones that they had to move together.

Plunking them down just right rounded out the perfect swimming hole for the Woodlanders. Several of them bounded over and dove in, hooting with delight. Soon it was filled with little, backstroking, breaststroking, floating swimmers, hollering thank-yous to Palmer and Samantha.

Tara and Elsa swam over to where Sam was resting on the large rocks.

"Isn't it the most perfect night?" Tara asked Samantha.

"Perfect," Sam agreed with a sigh.

Elsa swam in circles around her granddaughter, and they splashed one another before turning to splash Sam's feet. The cool water felt wonderful on her toes. She worried about the little bundle in her pocket getting wet, and decided it was a good time to share it with the Woodlanders.

"Elsa," asked Sam, "would you please gather everyone around? I have something for them." Samantha stood up and reached into her pocket. She carefully pulled out a small square parcel, made from two pieces of gray felt, stitched together with purple twine.

The nearest Woodlanders who saw it first exclaimed loudly, "An amber token! From far away!"

Within a moment they were all clamoring to get a closer look. Sam stepped onto the grass and sat down, with dozens of Woodlanders following her out of the stream, along with a curious Palmer. They grabbed some towels and patted each other dry.

They made a path for Walter as he came out of the water, dripping, toward Sam. She held out the parcel for him and he reached for it. It was the size of a bed pillow in his arms. Several lanterns were brought over for Walter to see better. Samantha spoke softly, explaining how she had come to find the amber token at camp.

"I couldn't get back to the twin pine to see if your amber token had been discovered by the Woodlanders there. We didn't hike in that part of the woods again. On the last day of camp, I was packing to go home. I went outside on the porch to get the birdhouse I had made in wood shop.

"There, just inside it, was this amber token. It had the same purple twine from the one you made, so I knew what it was. I knew that I was meant to bring it back here and give it to you." Sam finished her story and looked around at the tiny faces leaning in to hear every word.

"Open it!" pleaded Tara.

Walter untied the knots. Inside was a drawstring pouch made of green silk. Walter loosened it, reached inside and pulled out a handful of amber beads. They were square, unlike the round ones they were used to seeing. The unusual shape delighted the Woodlanders.

"They're so beautiful!" Tara exclaimed, taking one and holding it up to the lantern.

"Much darker than ours," added Marta. They

passed a few beads around the crowd and everyone admired them. Next, Walter removed a scroll of two pages of wood-pulp paper.

"There's a letter," he noted. Clearing his throat, waiting for silence, he read it aloud:

Dear Family,

We are so thankful for the lovely amber beads you sent for us. We will always treasure them. We hope you are as delighted by our own, different in shape but made with the same devotion. We have included a map of our woods. Yours is hanging in our Great Hall to much regard. You are all in our hearts, and we wish you Peace and Light.

It was signed by thirty or forty Woodlanders, Sam couldn't count them all. There were even some childlike scrawls. Walter passed the letter around for everyone to see, and opened the map. It was a work of art, depicting the pine forest, the lake, and nearby Camp Walden. There was a circle around Sam's cabin.

"How did they know which cabin was mine?" Sam asked.

Walter shrugged. "Woodlanders are always aware of their neighbors, their comings and goings."

Sam thought of the Woodlanders sneaking around the bunks at night while all the campers were sleeping. It made her smile.

The light from the lanterns grew dim as the oil burned low. Some cookies and punch were passed around, and everyone enjoyed a snack.

Palmer and Samantha helped the Woodlanders pack up their things. Only a few lanterns were still lit as they put on their little boots. Then they lined up between their Protectlings to head home, exhausted and happy. It was a slower march back to the beech tree.

After seeing the last of the Woodlanders safely into the roots of the great tree, Sam and Palmer found their way back to the trail. They walked side by side in silence. Where the trail split, Palmer stopped before heading off toward his own yard.

"I'm glad you're home, Sam," said Palmer, reaching over and yanking gently on her ponytail.

She batted his hand away, and gave him a shove. "Me too," she replied, turning to leave. "I missed the Woodlanders, and you," she added, jogging off into the dark. Palmer watched her disappear. He smiled before sprinting toward home.

Samantha crawled into bed that night with pruned feet. She reached for her sketchbook and pencils. It was hard to choose something to draw from the celebration at the stream. She wished she could make a painting of it all.

Instead she put her pencil to the paper, and watched as the Woodlanders' circle of light appeared. She shaded the dark all around it, and left the center white, to look like it was glowing. She drew a large quote bubble above the circle, and filled it in with three words: Be The Light. I think that's what Elsa said, she thought, sleepily. She couldn't remember exactly. It didn't matter. She understood.

★　★　★

It was now August 1965, and Martin and Jack drove in silence. They knew that the farmhouse was empty. Norman's daughter had come from Chicago last week to collect her father and his things. Movers emptied the rest of the house shortly after. Still, the two men were cautious to remain unseen as the afternoon light faded. They didn't run into anyone on the gravel road. Jack parked the Mustang near the porch steps. Getting out of the car, they both looked at the vacant house. In the fading light, it looked a bit shabby, but solid.

"Such a pretty old place," said Jack. "It's a shame to tear it down. Lots of charm."

Martin scowled, shaking his head. "It's a dump," he responded. "That barn over there is dangerous, could collapse at any minute. I think we can sell those old beams in it. They weigh a ton!"

"Whatever," Jack said. Martin was always scheming to get one more dime. It was hard to keep up with him.

"Let's get this over with, before someone sees us," Martin mumbled.

Jack's stomach sank as Martin shook a brown paper sack in his direction. Jack wanted to run away, because he knew what was inside the bag: a half-smoked cigar and a book of matches from Norm's favorite seed store. He closed his eyes and rubbed at the lines between his brows before following Martin across the field toward the woods, lumbering behind him with heavy steps.

★ ★ ★

Just inside the forest, young Walter and his father hiked along the deer path. They were venturing farther than the boy had ever gone before. It was dangerous for Woodlanders to be on their own, without a Protectling, but this was a rite of passage. Walter was old enough now to practice the skills this required: quiet steps, alert ears, and eagle eyes. Modeling himself after Henry, Walter moved along the trail with confidence. They were eager to set up camp inside an old log near Woods Edge before darkness fell.

"There, next to the stone wall," Henry pointed to a fallen oak covered with brambles, snuggled up against the wall that bordered the field. "Perfect shelter for the night," he added.

Walter bounded ahead to check it out. He

approached the stone wall, dropping his pack and scaling the first rock with ease. He rested his foot in a crevice, glancing back at Henry for permission.

"Careful," his dad advised with a nod. "Secure your footing and test your grip. We have about thirty minutes of light left, so take a quick peek over the top and then climb back down to help me set up camp. We can explore in the morning."

Walter had climbed up the next stone before Henry's warning was done. Two smaller rocks were easier and within a minute he was on top of the old stone wall. He stood straight as an arrow, hands on his hips. "Coo roo, coo roo," he called back to Henry, mimicking the call of a mourning dove.

Henry returned the call: "Coo roo..." It was their 'All is well' message.

Stretching his neck, Walter took in the view. Dusk was settling over the field. He longed to jump down and run through the pasture.

Suddenly, some movement by the farmhouse caught his eye and he turned quickly to check it out.

Too quickly—before he could warn Henry about the two Dumans headed across the field toward the woods, Walter lost his footing and tumbled head first over the wall.

Henry heard Walter shriek and looked up with alarm to see him fall, and disappear over the side.

"Walter!" gasped Henry, scrambling over and

clawing his way up the rocks. He collapsed onto his stomach on top of the wall, clambering to the edge. Looking over it, he saw Walter below, crumpled against a stone, unmoving. At the same moment, he saw what had distracted his son: two men walking toward the woods, their path leading them directly to Walter.

Henry froze. He looked up at the men, then down at Walter. His mind was spinning. Perhaps the men wouldn't notice the tiny boy in the settling darkness. He was not moving, and his clothing was brown and gray.

Henry thought that if he tried to get to Walter now they would see the movement for certain, so he chose to slip back over the wall. There was a tiny ledge on the next rock down where he stopped. He sat there helpless and filled with dread. He took a deep breath, hoping that the men's path would change enough to lead them in another direction.

He could hear them now. They were arguing, stomping closer. Their steps swished through the tall grass, muffling their voices. They stopped several feet away from the stone wall. Henry listened, certain that it was best to remain unseen.

He waited for them to pass by, clenching and unclenching his fists. The two men seemed intent on some task. It was obvious to Henry that they were not out for an evening nature hike.

"Enough of your whining, Jack," one of them said in clear frustration and anger. "It'll be dark in a few minutes—it's time to get this done." A paper bag rustled between them.

"Give it to me, Martin," a deeper voice demanded, without much authority. "We're not going to do this! It's not right. Someone could get hurt, the animals and birds ..." The bag ripped.

"Darn, Jack, let go! Get back to the car, then, and start it up. I'll do this myself." The angry one seemed to be in charge, giving orders like he was talking to a naughty child.

Just then, Henry heard some movement close by him on the other side of the wall. He hoped the two men had not heard it as well. It sounded like Walter was stirring. Relief swelled within Henry but was quickly replaced by panic. He held his breath and wished Walter would be still and quiet. His heart pounded when he heard small moans and whimpers.

The men heard it as well. "What was that?" the deeper voice whispered. Their footsteps moved closer.

"One of your precious birds or chipmunks—I think it's hurt," the other one murmured. Henry could hear them approaching Walter. They had seen him, he was certain. There was nothing he could do now to help him. Cringing, he gathered his wits as best he could. He knew that any chance he might have to save Walter depended upon remaining unseen. It took all of his strength to be calm. The urge to run out of hiding to help his son was overwhelming, but he listened and *waited.*

Walter sat up at the sound of voices. His vision was blurry, but he saw two large figures approaching him. There was nowhere to hide, and his head was hurting badly, so he remained still. He wanted to call out to his father but decided not to speak at all. Fear sank in his belly, chilling his whole body.

"It's not an animal, it's a toy, or doll or something," the larger man said, bending over Walter. "Some of them make sounds if you pull a string," he added, kneeling down and reaching for Walter.

In terror, the boy squirmed out of Jack's reach, squeezing himself into a crevice between the stones. Both men fell back in alarm and shock.

"It's not a toy!" Exclaimed the short one, crawling closer on all fours. "It's alive," he whispered in disbelief. Martin's mouth hung open as he squinted down at Walter.

"Give me those matches—I can't see it very well." He extended his hand over to Jack without taking his eyes off Walter. Jack fumbled with the bag Martin had dropped. Shakily, he found the matches and struck one.

"Careful," he said, handing it over to Martin. "He looks real scared." Martin took it and slowly brought the flame down and held it a few inches away from Walter.

"It's a tiny boy," Martin murmured, amazed at the illuminated face before him. Walter blinked up at them.

He was afraid of the one holding the match.

Walter decided to take advantage of the settling darkness, hoping that his dad was nearby, ready to help him. With all his might, he sprang forward, blew out the match and spun around to scale the wall as fast as he could.

"Grab him!" Martin shouted to Jack. They both scrambled, pouncing on the small figure.

Walter was dizzy from bumping his head. It slowed him down and made it easy for the men to capture him.

"Got him," Jack declared, closing his large hands around the tiny being. Walter's head poked out of the space between Jack's thumbs, and his little knees were pinned to his chest inside the hollow fist. He pushed as hard as he could against the palms that surrounded him. Jack squeezed tighter, and Walter gave up the fight.

Jack brought his hands up close to his face, but it was difficult to see anything in the fading light. Martin stepped closer, reaching toward Walter with an extended finger. The boy's head withdrew, and Jack moved his hands close to his chest.

"You're scaring him," Jack complained, turning away from Martin. Holding Walter carefully, he walked away from the wall and headed toward the field.

"Stop! Where are you going?" Martin grabbed onto the back of Jack's shirt. "Do you realize what we've found here?" He was talking fast. Jack paused and

turned to face him. He didn't have a plan, but knew that he should keep the boy out of Martin's reach.

Henry climbed over the wall as quietly as he could. Lying flat, he could see the two figures outlined in the rising moonlight. Soon the moon would be bright, but for now he was grateful for the darkness as he scaled down the rocks onto the ground below, ready to follow them.

"Let's just get him to the barn for now," the angry one said. "I saw some old groundhog traps in there. We could keep him in one while we figure out what to do." He was calmer now, encouraging the big man to listen.

Henry could see the taller one nod in agreement, and they both set off into the field. He ran along behind them, their footprints in the tall grass aiding his speed, and their bickering voices covering any sounds from his little boots.

"We could make a fortune!" exclaimed Martin. He was having a hard time keeping up with Jack's long stride. He kept talking louder and faster. Jack walked on, gently cradling Walter in his hands.

"People would pay to see him," Martin continued. "We could build a little place for him with open walls like a dollhouse. I bet he has a mother and father back there, and sisters and brothers. We could capture them all—"

"He's a person, Martin, not an animal," Jack said quietly. He was trying to figure out how to get away from Martin. Perhaps he could drive off with the little guy in the Mustang and leave Martin behind.

Jack knew that he had to do something to stop Martin, but his mind was blank. For now, he decided to play along, until he could come up with a plan. He was intent on saving the boy. Any others like him were in danger as well with Martin hunting for them.

They approached the barn. Its large door hung crookedly on old rails. Jack stepped aside and motioned for Martin to open it. He tried but struggled, unable to make it budge more than a few inches.

"It's stuck," Martin complained, giving up. Jack did not intend to hand over the boy. He put his foot into the gap and pushed it open with his leg, and used his shoulder to glide it along its tracks. The whole building creaked and groaned. A small slat of wood from the ceiling crashed down inside. Stale scents of hay and manure escaped and surrounded them.

"Yuck," said Martin, wincing. He spat on the ground. Fumbling along the wall inside, he found a light switch and flipped it. One bare bulb came on over their heads. Beyond its feeble glow, the barn was speckled with moonlight from the cracks and holes in its walls and roof.

Henry was a few minutes behind, but he could see them in the light of the old barn's doorway. He stayed in the shadows, waiting for the men to turn away before moving any closer. The large man's hands were not visible, so he wasn't sure if Walter was still in his grasp.

"The traps are by that wall over there," Martin gestured, disappearing into a horse stall. He emerged carrying a wire cage, and placed it at Jack's feet. They both stared at it, unsure how to open it. Martin kicked it, then banged on its sides and pulled at it. Finally, a latch released.

Slowly, Jack opened his hands to have a look at the boy. Walter tried to jump out, but Jack caught him against his chest.

"Careful!" Martin warned. "Get him in here," he said, holding open the cage door. Jack brought his hands down close to the ground and quickly pushed Walter inside the trap, slamming it shut. Walter stumbled in and retreated to its corner, sitting with his knees pulled up closely against his chest. He rested his head on his knees, face down, avoiding the Dumans' stares. They were now on their hands and knees, peering at him.

"I can't believe what I'm seeing," Martin whispered. "A miniature person, what do you think, four inches tall?" He turned to look at Jack, who nodded in agreement, speechless.

Martin continued. "Let's get him some food and water, and leave him in the barn for tonight. I don't think it's a good idea to tell anyone else about him, until we have a plan."

Jack worried about Martin's plans. "I'll stay here with him, you can go home," he replied, keeping his eyes on the boy.

Martin looked over at Jack, watching him scoot closer to the cage. He wondered what Jack was thinking. Leaving him here alone with the boy didn't seem wise. Martin stood up and walked over to a bench by the door. He sat down, crossed his legs and folded his arms.

"Okay, then. I guess we should both stay, and come up with a plan together," Martin said, leaning back against the wall. He smiled at Jack, but Jack did not smile back.

"There's a box of crackers in the car," Martin remembered. "Let's see if he wants some." He got up and walked out into the night.

Henry crouched outside in the tall hickory weeds growing near the barn door. When the smaller man emerged and headed toward the car, Henry dashed inside the barn, crawling along the shadows against the wall. The large man was sitting next to a cage on the floor, uneasy in his posture. He lifted his head and glanced over as Henry scuttled in, but didn't see him. There was a flat-nosed shovel propped against the wall nearby, and Henry hid behind its spade. Peeking out, he could see Walter several feet away in the cage. Henry was relieved that his son seemed unharmed.

"I can hear mice crawling around in here, I bet there are lots of them now that the cats are gone," Jack said softly to Walter. "How old are you, kid?"

Walter raised his head but did not reply. Out of the corner of his eye, he saw some movement behind the shovel near the door. His father's face peeked out from behind it, and then retreated. Seeing Henry, Walter relaxed a bit. He stretched his legs out in front of him, feeling that everything would now be all right somehow.

Martin returned from the car and sat down next to Jack, his back to the barn door.

"I don't think he talks," Jack informed Martin. "Or, maybe his language is different, but he won't answer me." He took the snack box from Martin and opened it. He poked a few crackers through the wire cage. Walter watched the pieces land at his feet, but he wasn't hungry.

A sudden crashing noise near the door startled them. The men jumped up, and Walter stood in his cage. The shovel had fallen over, banging noisily to the ground. Walter strained to see Henry, but he was gone. He looked right and left but saw no sign of him.

"What was that?" asked Martin, wide-eyed.

"Who's there?" Jack shouted out into the night. Only a few crickets responded. The men exhaled loudly and walked toward the door, looking out into the dark field.

"Let's close this," Martin said, grabbing the long handle and pushing the door along the rail. It moved a few inches before going no farther. He struggled for a minute before Jack took over.

"It's stuck," he complained. "The track is messed up." Jack pushed and pulled at it, grunting with strain. In frustration, he rammed the door with his huge shoulder. It still wouldn't budge, so he put his full strength into it, and rammed it again. The wood creaked above their heads as the door finally slid along its track. Jack slammed it shut.

At first, it sounded like rusty hinges were groaning above their heads. Martin looked at Jack, confused by the noise. Then he realized what was happening, and lunged for the door. One large beam from the other end of the barn came crashing down, followed by another. The ceiling was collapsing.

"I can't open it! You try!" Martin hollered. He ran over and grabbed the cage, sprinting back over to where Jack struggled with the door. Another beam fell, smashing the horse stall into bits.

"It won't move!" Jack yelled, pulling at it with all his might. Hay dust was billowing, causing them to wheeze and cough. Panicked, Martin dropped the cage. It fell on its side, tumbling Walter within it. The men struggled in vain with the giant door. Two more enormous beams crashed down, bringing the rest of the roof with them. It sounded like fireworks as windows broke and wood cracked and split around them.

In a minute, it was all over. Dust swirled up into the night sky, and silence settled around the rubble.

Walter was okay. The old trap had protected him. He sneezed, covered in hay dust and splintered wood. He listened for sounds of the men, or Henry, but heard nothing. Sputtering grime from his mouth, he wondered what he should do next. Then, he heard the call of a mourning dove.

"Coo roo, Coo roo." It was Henry, calling to him with their secret signal. With relief, he returned the call, and waited. He couldn't see anything but smashed wood in the moonlight in gaps around and above the cage.

The call came again, closer this time. He returned it, and waited again. Henry was using the call to locate him. He heard rustling nearby, and turned toward it in the dark. "Coo roo," he repeated. Then, he saw Henry's shadow, squeezing between two boards above the cage. He landed on top of it, then climbed down, reaching inside to hold Walter's hand in his own.

Walter started to speak, but Henry shushed him, urging him to be silent. He worked his way around to the trap door, which was on the side of the cage now. The latch opened easily, just enough space for Walter to squeeze through and embrace his father.

There weren't any open spaces along the ground, so they climbed through the debris above the cage as best they could. It took a long time. On top of it at last, they sat on a beam in the moonlight, resting. The grass of the field rolled in the breeze in front of them, like waves on water. A clear path could be seen through it to the woods where the men had walked at dusk.

"Are they dead?" Walter whispered to Henry.

"I'm not sure," Henry responded. "We need to find out. Someone will come looking for them. If they are alive, we need to make sure they don't remember finding you."

Just then, they heard a moan from the rubble below. Pieces of wood shifted and fell.

"Martin?" Jack called out in a pained voice. "Are you okay?" *There was no response at first, but then Martin groaned.*

"My legs are pinned—I can't move," answered Martin. "Where are you?" *It was clear they couldn't see each other.*

"I'm close by you," Jack responded. "I can't move either, my arm is stuck."

Henry and Walter looked at each other. This would buy them some time.

Henry leaned close to whisper in Walter's ear. "We will have to use Dreamguiding to change their memory. I know you have never done that before, but just follow my instructions and everything will be all right. I know you can do it," *Henry assured him.*

Walter nodded, even though he felt uncertain. He and his father turned their attention to the conversation below.

"Just sit tight," *Martin was saying.* "The surveyors

are coming in the morning to measure the housing lots. They'll be able to hear us," he was talking fast. "We'll be out of this mess before lunch, don't you worry, Jack."

"Where is the trap?" Jack asked. "Hey, kid? Are you okay?" he shouted from below. Wood creaked.

"Stop moving!" hissed Martin. "You have to be still or we could get crushed under here. It's not stable," he explained. "We're lucky to be alive." His voice trailed off.

Jack lay his head back down, but felt around the spaces near his free hand. Only splintered wood and dust, no cage. He gave up and closed his eyes.

Henry whispered to Walter. "We have to wait until they fall asleep," he told him. "Focus all your thoughts on being sleepy right now." He yawned silently and Walter copied him, surprised by his own need to yawn. Henry yawned again.

A loud, drawn-out yawn rose up from the rubble. Another one followed. Martin and Jack discussed their plan for the morning, which included hollering out to the surveyors so they could find them. Jack thought his arm was broken, and Martin worried that his leg might be broken as well. They were relieved not to notice any major bleeding except for some scratches. They itemized their injuries between yawns.

"I can't keep my eyes open," declared Jack.

Martin yawned back. "I'm drowsy, too. We might as well get some rest," he suggested.

Several minutes passed. "Wake me up if you hear anything, okay?" requested Martin. Jack responded with some heavy snoring. Soon a steady rhythm of snores bounced back and forth between them.

Henry leaned closer to his son. "Because they are strangers to us, we must be touching them during Dreamguiding," he explained to Walter. Together they made up a story to replace the events of the day and agreed on its details. Walter was unsure how Dreamguiding worked. He worried that they wouldn't have enough time.

"Be careful and quiet climbing down," Henry told him. "We don't want to wake them." Walter followed behind his father. The two of them found spaces between the broken pieces of wood, and moved toward the snoring sounds below. After a few minutes of downward plodding, they were close to the sleeping men.

Henry dropped to the ground next to Martin's knee and set to Dreamguiding. Walter found an opening near Jack's shoulder. He reached over and placed his hand on Jack's free arm. Then, he tried to pace his breathing to match Jack's, as Henry had told him. Just doing that relaxed him.

He closed his eyes and imagined the view into the woods from the farmhouse. Then, he pictured the stone wall ahead, and approached it in his imagination. He saw the twilight sky and heard the tall grass rustling in the breeze. Now, it became easy for him, like he was making up a story in his mind.

Walter continued with the plot he and Henry had planned. It included images of Jack and Martin finding an injured ferret by the wall. Jack carried it back to the barn, protecting it. Martin wanted to sell it to a pet store, but Jack said no. They put the ferret in a groundhog trap in the barn, but then the ceiling collapsed.

Walter opened his eyes after remembering the noisy, frightening scene. He waited patiently for the signal from Henry. When he heard the mourning dove call, he returned it softly, and then made his way out of the rubble. He was exhausted.

Henry searched the edges of the ruined barn for Walter. It was difficult to see much, but his son appeared, crawling out on his belly. He ran to help him up, and the two of them made their way across the gravel to the field.

Dirty and weak, they followed the trail in the grass that Martin and Jack had made, knowing it would lead them to their campsite at the wall.

"How will we know if the Dreamguiding worked?" Walter asked Henry. He wasn't sure he had done it right. Together, they climbed the wall, resting for a moment at the top.

"It always works," Henry assured him. "We created new memories that will replace the other ones. They won't forget what they felt, but we changed what they remember seeing. The new story we created will cover up the earlier one, and they will forget it." Henry sounded very tired, but Walter wanted to ask more questions.

"Who invented Dreamguiding?" Walter wondered. He knew that the Woodlanders used it to train Protectlings, but he hadn't known that it could be used to reshape memories.

"I'm not sure," Henry responded, as he helped Walter down the other side. "It has been passed down from generation to generation. The Dumans are capable of practicing it as well, but they are unaware of it."

"That's probably a good thing," Walter said, thinking about Martin.

"It's a very good thing," Henry agreed. Together they packed up their things and headed home to the beech tree.

SEPTEMBER

The morning was clear and cool. After the heavy heat of summer, Sam enjoyed the crisp air. She zipped up her polar fleece and took a deep breath as she squinted up at the sky. It was a perfect blue, and looked like it had milk in it. A few clouds drifted by. She made her way down Primrose Lane to catch the bus.

The bus stop was on Lily Lane. Sam waited there alone, wishing she had made plans to wait for Palmer. Just then, Palmer and Lulu appeared around the corner. She was relieved to see them. They were silent, trudging toward her with serious faces.

None of them had ever taken the bus before. This first day of middle school was going to be filled with new things.

"Hey," Palmer greeted Sam as he dropped his backpack next to hers on the sidewalk. Lulu added her green backpack to the pile.

"Did you bring your lunch or are you buying?" Lulu asked them, kicking a stone across the street. Palmer and Sam answered in unison: "Buying."

The conversation stopped there. Sighs and fidgeting overflowed from the three of them. Lulu jumped down from the curb, and then back up onto the sidewalk, over and over.

"Cut it out, Lu," Palmer begged. "You're driving me nuts!"

"You were already nuts," Lulu responded. She bounced a few more times before sitting down on the curb. They could hear the bus approaching, and turned to watch it chug up the hill.

Palmer handed Lulu her backpack, and then Sam's to her. He smiled at them both. She returned his smile as best she could.

The first day of school turned out to be exciting. Sam had a different teacher for each subject, which was unlike fifth grade. When the bell rang she had to leave one classroom and go to another one at the other end of the big school. No one lined up the kids and walked them around. They expected you to know where you were going. Sam hoped she would get the hang of it.

In the hallways, Sam had an uneasy feeling. She sensed someone was following her, and watching her at her locker when her back was turned. After closing it up, she warily scanned the crowd of students, but no one seemed to be looking her way. She shrugged and merged into the line of shuffling feet towards her next class.

By two o'clock she was tired. Sitting in one

place for fifty minutes made her drowsy, so she started doodling pictures of the Woodlander's Butternut Harvest. Looking forward to it was a welcome distraction.

The ring of the bell shocked her attention back into the classroom. She realized that she hadn't heard anything the teacher said about homework. Good thing they posted the assignments online, she thought to herself.

Packing up her things along with the rest of the kids, she headed for the bus. Lulu and Palmer were waiting by her locker. They were relaxed and laughing, which was a big improvement from the last time she had seen them in the cafeteria at lunchtime. The three of them walked to the bus together. They didn't say much, but Sam could tell that the first day of middle school had gone well for her friends.

At home, Sam went online to get her homework assignments. Then she grabbed an apple and a brown paper shopping bag and headed outside to gather some sticks and twigs for the Woodlanders' fires.

The Butternut Harvest took three days. The first night was just a party, really. The Woodlanders feasted at tables filled with all their favorite butternut foods—soups, breads, puddings and cookies. It smelled wonderful. They didn't need a Protectling there for the feast in the Great Hall, but

Samantha brought in some wood and usually stayed awhile. There was music and storytelling by the fire.

The next morning, the Woodlanders would clean out the nut bin, the large chamber where they stored the nuts. It was almost as big as the Great Hall, large enough to hold a year's supply of butternuts. There were only a few dozen nuts left now. The last of them would be used up for the feast.

One of Sam's jobs was to uncover the small hatch over the bin and make sure the chute below it was open. It was buried in a year's worth of dirt now, and the area around it needed to be clear, so that the Woodlanders could roll nuts to it and push them down the chute. They could access the bin from the mill in the homestead.

It took almost an entire day to fill the bin. Four old white walnut trees that produced heaps of butternuts surrounded the hatch. It was in the middle of a small, sunny field not far from the beech tree. Sam was going to start clearing the area today.

The afternoon had grown chilly, so Sam zipped up her fleece. She picked up fat twigs for firewood along the path on her way to the butternut field. Taking a big bite from her apple, she stuffed sticks into the paper bag she had brought from the kitchen. She stopped chewing and looked behind her. The feeling from earlier in the hallways at school returned. She saw no one there, but she felt like someone was following her. Turning around in a circle, Sam peered between the trees and around the bushes. Seeing nothing, she bent to gather more firewood.

Sam was looking forward to the part of the feast when the Woodlanders sang about how every nut had the potential to become a tree. They always left one behind on a special rock, as a nod of thanks. They used up the last of their store for their celebration, knowing that there would be plenty for them in the next season.

She was humming the melody of the Harvest Hymn when she heard footsteps behind her. Nervously, she turned around, and was startled to see a familiar face. She couldn't place where she had seen it before. It was a girl, standing on the trail, wearing a black knit hat and a green sweater. She stepped toward Sam and snatched the paper bag out of Sam's hands.

"Hey, Slowpoke Sam," the girl blurted out. "What are you up to out here all by yourself?"

It was Maddie. Sam didn't recognize her at first with her hair covered. At camp she was always in braids and tee shirts. With a sigh, Sam tossed her apple core off the trail and crossed her arms. She wondered what Maddie was doing here. Didn't she live in Connecticut?

"Sticks?" Maddie humphed, peering into the bag. "You're so weird. I saw you at my new school today but you didn't notice me. Then it became a really fun game to spy on you in the hall. I could tell it was freaking you out!" Maddie laughed loudly. It echoed through the quiet woods, spoiling the peaceful afternoon.

Sam looked at her with curiosity. Now it seemed like she wouldn't be able to gather the rest of the firewood. Maddie was dumping the sticks out and stomping on them.

"I was going to build something with those," Sam said, grabbing back the empty paper bag. "Why are you here? Don't you live in Hartford?" she asked impatiently.

"We moved last week," Maddie told her. "The schools are better here. Too bad we don't have any classes together," she said, looking at Sam with interest. "Maybe we can have lunch together tomorrow," Maddie added.

Was she serious? Sam started walking towards home, hoping that Maddie would follow her back to the neighborhood, away from the beech tree.

"Where's your new house?" Sam asked.

Maddie ran to catch up with her. "We live on Lavender Lane, number ten," she answered. "I know you live on Primrose Lane, number twenty-five," Maddie told her. "I saw you leaving for the bus stop today when my mom drove me to school.

Tomorrow I'll take the bus, too."

Sam wondered why Maddie hadn't taken the bus this morning. Maybe she had been too nervous. This thought made Sam feel less frustrated with her.

As they approached the gate into Sam's yard, Maddie continued to follow her. Sam wanted to get back to the beech tree to help the Woodlanders prepare for the Butternut Harvest, but her mother saw them from the yard and invited Maddie to stay for dinner.

Sam ended up missing the whole Butternut Harvest. Her grandparents came the next day and stayed for the weekend. The next week she had lots of homework. There was no free time to get to the woods.

A few weeks later when she met up with Tom and Marta for another nighttime trek to the

Morley's, she was relieved to hear that the Harvest was wonderful. Perfect in every way. They hadn't needed her. Her relief was mixed with something else she couldn't name, but it felt a little like being lost.

★　★　★

By September 1965, the work on the Rawlings Meadow development had started. Jack limped along the edge of the woods carefully. His foot was sprained, and his arm was in a cast. He used a cane for support. Near the stone wall, he turned to look across the field to the pile of rubble that used to be the barn. A few large cranes and bulldozers worked noisily to clean it all up.

He wondered what had happened to the injured black-footed ferret he and Martin had found here. When the surveyors had rescued them in the morning, the wire trap had been empty.

Martin and Jack had spent a day in the hospital after they were found under the collapsed barn. They knew they were lucky to be alive. Martin had suffered a broken leg and a few cracked ribs.

Finding that ferret had distracted them from Martin's plan to burn down the woods. At first, Jack worried that Martin would want to hobble back out here on his crutches and set the fire. But something had changed his mind. He told Jack that the night they were trapped, he had dreamt about the woods. He couldn't remember it exactly, but he woke up certain that old Norm was right.

Jack bent down to retrieve a ripped paper bag next to the stone wall. He turned and watched the bulldozers make another pile of rubble out of the farmhouse. They moved forward, crashing into walls and tumbling them down, then backing up and attacking the next one.

He was glad they had found that ferret. Jack was planning to live in the new neighborhood himself, right here on the edge of the woods. He felt calm here. The woods were alive with energy, harmonious and peaceful. He wondered perhaps if that's what Martin had seen in his dream.

OCTOBER

Marta sat up in her feather bed, rubbing her eyes and stretching her arms overhead. She looked around the cozy room, wondering when Tom had risen. He had left her a cup of peppermint tea in an acorn cup, still warm on the nightstand. She sipped it, enjoying its sweetness. Her stomach rumbled. Tom would be waiting to have breakfast with her, so she stepped into her felt slippers and made her way to the kitchen.

"Good morning, my dear," Tom greeted her. "I'm so glad to see you looking well rested." He pulled a chair out from the table for her and kissed the top of her head as she settled into it. Tara sat at the other end of the table, already dressed. She smiled at her mother.

A birthday party for Marta's mother, Elsa, was planned for that evening. Walter had invited everyone to the Great Hall for music and cake. Marta was certain it would be a bigger celebration than that. Elsa was a beloved leader next to Walter, adored for her nurturing care of all the

Woodlanders. She was a gifted healer with knowledge of herbs and treatments, tending fevers, stitching cuts, splinting and casting broken bones. She was now busy each day teaching Tara all she knew. The two of them were very close. It made Marta happy to see her daughter growing up into such a caring, skillful young woman.

Tara excused herself from the table, kissing each parent on the forehead.

"I'm off to inventory Grand Mum's supplies with her," she explained. Marta blew her a kiss in return.

"We'll be decorating the Great Hall for the party after lunch if you want to join us," her mother told her.

"Fun! I'll see you there," Tara promised, as she headed out of the kitchen and into their cozy front room. It would be chilly in the corridors, so she grabbed her coat off a hook by the door.

It would take five minutes or so to walk through the tunnels to the Infirmary. Without a lantern, they were mostly dark, except for shafts of light that came from hollow trees above. Tara was not afraid. She could find her way with her eyes closed. The Infirmary was directly below a hollow twin pine, so it was warmly lit during the day.

Entering Elsa's workspace delighted Tara. She found her grandmother writing at her large oak desk.

"Happy Birthday, Grand Mum!" Tara sang, approaching her with open arms. They embraced each other in a warm hug.

"It has been a happy one so far, now even better with your warm wishes," Elsa smiled, releasing Tara and tapping her on the nose with her index finger.

Tara adored her grandmother. The two of them shared a delight in the same things: botany, books, watercolors, and butternut bread pudding.

Everyday clothes for Elsa included a muslin apron with a pair of linen work gloves tucked into the front pocket. She wore a necklace of amber beads around her neck, a cherished gift from Walter. Her gray hair was always pulled into a messy updo, which perfectly framed her round face and twinkling, emerald eyes.

"I was just taking a look at our supplies," Elsa explained, waving a hand at the wall of shelves behind her. Dozens of imperfectly shaped jars with cork lids filled each row.

"I'm afraid I broke the jar of feverfew and bloodroot," Elsa frowned. "It might be too late in the season to gather more."

Tara nodded. "That's okay, we'll make do." She knew where she could find the herbs, but the broken jar was a problem. Glassblowing was a big project that took weeks, resulting in the production of only a dozen jars and lanterns. These precious items were always in low supply and high demand.

The next hour flew by quickly as they worked together in easy order. Tara carefully checked each jar and its contents. After many seasons at this task, she knew all the different herbs and their uses.

"Witch hazel and elder flower," Tara read off one label. "Full jar," she informed Elsa, who then recorded this information carefully in a large ledger.

"This combination is useful for ... ?" quizzed Elsa patiently. She was pleased by Tara's quick and certain responses.

"The treatment of minor burns," Tara replied. "Tea applied to clean linen and placed directly on the skin. A new dressing should be applied every three hours for two days." Tara spoke without hesitation. She had worked hard to learn every treatment and was confident in her knowledge.

"Well done, Tara," observed Elsa. "I'm grateful for your help and company. You honor us all with your effort and devotion. Let's get some lunch. I have acorn soup and goldenrod bread at the hearth."

Tara considered the invitation. "Thanks, Grand Mum, but Mom and Dad are expecting me. You go on and I'll see you tonight at the party."

Tara grabbed an empty basket off the shelf as they left the Infirmary together. Elsa thought it was odd that Tara headed toward the Great Hall instead of joining her in the direction of the private quarters. Some birthday party mission perhaps. Elsa was too humble to ask about the celebration, so she dismissed her curiosity. Had she known Tara's plan, she would have stopped her for certain. They parted with a hug and went their separate ways.

Tara climbed the curving staircase in the Great Hall up to the double doors. Lifting the heavy latch, she breathed in the crisp air. Closing the door behind her, she stepped out from under the roots of the sheltering tree, wiping away a sticky spider's web that clung to her face as she moved out into the light. She took a moment to bundle her scarf against the chill.

She knew it wasn't a good idea to venture out alone. The Woodlanders rarely did. However, Tara wanted to collect the last bits of bloodroot and feverfew before the frost. A basketful would please Elsa for her birthday. Winter always brought sore throats and fevers, best treated by the teas and tonics she made from these plants. There would be enough of them nearby under the leaves in the mossy shade. Tara knew she wouldn't have to look far.

Sunlight dappled the ground, creating patches of brilliance around her. Most of the leaves were down by now. They crunched beneath her feet in a deep carpet of maple, oak, and beech.

A powerful gust of wind blustered up from behind, knocking her onto her hands and knees.

Tara enjoyed the tumble, protected by a cushioning blanket of damp foliage. In a playful mood, she rolled onto her back and lay there, pleased by the comfort and charmed by the soaring branches and traces of sky above her. A few moments passed before she recalled her errand and looked around for her dropped basket. It was on its side in front of her. She sat up to brush the leaf bits from her sweater, feeling the need to return to the safety of the beech tree.

It was too late. From behind her, she heard two beats of great wings coming near. Before she could turn around, she felt sharp talons pierce her shoulders. Two more beats and she was up, rising toward the highest branches of the tallest trees, gripped in the claws of a strong bird of prey.

Was it a hawk, an owl? She couldn't see. Her stomach turned, dipped and tumbled. The bird struggled between the pines and oaks. It picked up speed in the clearings. Tara's eyes watered from the wind in her face. The pain in her neck and shoulders seared hot and throbbing. Her legs dangled beneath her, running against no ground. She realized that the bird, although three times her size, was having trouble holding onto her wriggling weight. This filled her frantic mind with a plan.

A burst of energy pulsed through her veins. She twisted her body with all her might, kicking her legs and thrashing her arms with the force of a storm.

Suddenly, the claws released her, and she dropped like a stone. It seemed a long way down, and her body somersaulted two whole turns. She worried for a split second about landing on her head, onto rocks or logs. Then the ground seemed to rush up to grab her and the world went dark and silent.

★ ★ ★

On Primrose Lane, inside for the whole morning, Samantha was restless. She cleaned her room and finished her chores around the house. Then she babysat Jared. Sitting in the window seat, she read *Anne of Green Gables*. Jared was busy at her feet setting up a roadway for his toy cars. Occasionally, he asked for her help solving construction problems on the floor.

Sam's grandparents were coming for dinner since it was Halloween, along with Uncle Paul and Aunt Beth. Samantha was excited to see the twins. Her cousins, Oliver and Paige, were the cutest babies she had ever seen. She couldn't wait to see their costumes. Her special connection with them was a secret, one she thought about for a moment while Jared built a miniature garage with his blocks.

Oliver and Paige would be Protectlings, just like herself. She tried to picture them at her age, walking through the dark woods at night. She wondered why Jared would not be a Protectling. There were never any training sessions with him here after he was born. Perhaps that was because Marta and Tom were busy training her for so many years. She tried to remember the sessions, but couldn't. Suddenly, her mind became a slide show of other memories.

She recalled her first meeting with Marta and Tom. It was after her eighth birthday, in the spring. She was exploring alone in the woods, and felt drawn to venture off the trail. She heard some faint laughter ahead, and picked up her pace toward it.

Suddenly, the most magnificent tree loomed before her. She had never been in this part of the woods, but the tree was familiar to her. Sitting near its roots, two tiny figures rested in the moss. She recognized them. From where? She didn't know, but it was obvious that they knew her as well.

The tiny man stood, offering his hand to help up his companion. Standing, they were only as tall as the youngest fern nearby.

Samantha greeted them by name, surprising herself. "Marta, Tom?" Sam questioned. She was not surprised that they knew her name as well.

"Samantha, thank you for joining us. We have been expecting you," Marta smiled warmly.

Tom added, "The three of us have worked hard, preparing together for this day, haven't we?"

"Yes, we have," Samantha replied, with an understanding that seemed to be gathering from somewhere deep inside her. She felt an affection for these two, and felt responsible for their care and protection.

"We don't have any duties for you today," Tom explained. "We just wanted you to see the place you have visited so many times in your dreams. We are grateful for your willingness to be a Protectling."

She knew exactly what that word meant, although she'd never heard it before. His small bow toward her filled the moment with warmth and importance.

Samantha recalled that the conversation

included some simple instructions about communication with the Woodlanders. Mostly she remembered not wanting to leave them. She had headed home with a sense of purpose and excitement. She couldn't wait to watch over them soon as they worked to complete their spring chores.

Enjoying these memories, Sam listened to Jared's buzzing sound effects as he hopped from one roadway to another.

Suddenly, she became aware of an urgent summons from the Woodlanders. It started as an ache in her chest, a sort of tugging at her heart. She understood it as a message to get to the beech tree right away.

She knew that meant waiting for her parents to return. The Woodlanders taught her that she was never to abandon her present responsibilities. She watched the clock, as time passed slowly, waiting.

An hour later, her parents arrived home. Sam helped them unload and put away the groceries. Then she had to help Jared put away what seemed like a million blocks and toy cars. Finally, her dad gave her the okay to head outside for some free time on her own. Grabbing her coat and backpack, she made her way out the door and headed to the woods as fast as her feet would carry her.

Something was wrong at the homestead—she could sense this with certainty. By the time she reached the beech tree, worry filled her mind like a buzzing alarm. She quickly uncovered the hatch door, stepped inside, and descended the ladder. In her haste she'd forgotten to shut the door and had to climb back up to secure it.

She jumped all the way down, landing in a heap at the corridor entrance to the Great Hall. She could hear voices there and crawled towards them.

"There is nothing else we can do right now, Dear." Walter was comforting Marta. She looked up to see Samantha entering the room. A mixture of relief and despair rippled across her face as she ran over to greet her.

"Samantha! I'm so grateful you came. Tara is missing."

Samantha tried to process this information, but felt confused.

Marta closed her eyes and took a deep breath before continuing. "She was supposed to help us set up for the birthday party, but no one can find her. She would not have gone out alone, would she?" She turned to Walter, but he didn't have any answers.

He addressed Sam. "We have searched the homestead but need you to begin a search of the woods west of the beech tree," Walter told her. "Tom is out already with Palmer, heading east."

Sam nodded, and agreed to check back with them in an hour.

"We will stay here and wait for you, in case she comes back, or Tom returns with any news," Walter frowned. His brow was furrowed, but he managed a slim smile of encouragement.

Sam nodded, turned toward the corridor and began the crawl back to the ladder. Standing at its foot, she took out her hat and gloves from her backpack and put them on before zipping up her coat. She secured the pack tightly on her back with a tug at the strap that fastened at her waist. Bounding up the ladder two steps at time, she pushed open the hatch and had it closed and covered in seconds.

The sky above was cloudy and gray. Sam looked for the sun to help her determine east from west, but couldn't find its glow. Besides, it would be directly above at this time of day, which wouldn't help much.

She approached the giant beech. The Woodlanders had taught her that moss grows thickest on the north side of trees. She walked around its base until it was obvious: heaps of spongy moss were definitely bulkier on one side. Turning around with the mossy bark at her back, she knew she was facing north, so she headed left to explore the west end of the woods. She set off, feeling a mix of fear and resolve. It was chilly, and Tara had possibly been out here for hours. Sam prayed that she would find her soon.

Then the fearful thoughts began. If Tara were all right, she would have made her way home by now. She knew the woods well and would never get lost. Furthermore, she knew not to set off alone in the first place.

Samantha tried to dismiss these hunches, as they filled her with worry. Tara must be hurt. She decided to leave it at that and focused on the ground around each one of her careful steps. There, almost invisible in the fallen leaves, she found a tiny hand-woven basket, about the size of a walnut in its shell.

★　★　★

Far from the beech tree on the other side of the woods, Tara was fitfully dreaming of tumbling through the air. Falling, then flying, then falling again. The odd images started to fade, replaced by an awareness of her own labored breathing.

A sharp pain caused Tara to open her eyes to muted, brownish light. The smell was familiar, and comforting: leaves, freshly fallen and damp. She was lying on her back, hesitant to move. Her whole body hurt.

Reaching up, she cleared away some leaves and breathed deeply. Hunger pains hummed in her belly. She watched the clouds move across a gray sky. Her left arm was the source of the sharp pain. Any time she tried to move it, she cried out in agony.

Tara used her right arm to push herself up into a sitting position. Her head barely peeked out from a pile of leaves. How did she get here, she wondered? She was grateful for the warmth and softness. Still, she was certain her arm was broken, and her head was throbbing. Her shoulders ached with every breath. She couldn't decide what to do. Mostly, she just wanted to lie back down and go to sleep. The sound of trickling water nearby soothed her pain and called her to rest. Letting her heavy eyelids close, Tara gave in to the soft bed of leaves.

A brown rabbit watched her from the bushes. As Tara's small head disappeared beneath the pile, he bounded toward her. Skirting around the leaves, he kicked them to cover her completely, out of view from hungry hunters in the sky.

★   ★   ★

Back at the beech tree, Samantha handled the tiny basket. An explanation for Tara's absence began to bubble up in her mind, and she didn't like it. Some hungry animal might have carried her off, or something had frightened her into hiding. Samantha called out Tara's name softly in each direction. Only the wind and creaking tree limbs answered her. She tucked the basket into her pocket.

She had a hunch that she should move on

toward the creek. The Woodlanders had taught her to tune into these inklings. They were always meaningful. Samantha trusted this magnetic message and followed its lead.

She walked for a while before reaching the creek, and then explored along it, searching, calling, and battling gloomy thoughts. It would be time to return to the beech tree soon without news or discovery, except for the basket. The temperature was dropping as the afternoon passed. Soon darkness would filter through the trees and veil the woods in black.

Samantha sat down to rest on a lichen-covered log next to the creek. Her murky mood was making her weak and tired. Shaking her head helped to clear it a bit.

A blurred movement by the bushes caught her eye and roused her curiosity. It was a brown rabbit, darting across the open spaces between the trees in front of her. She watched it sprint and hide, back and forth, four times.

Sam realized that the animal was nearing her perch on the log, so she placed her right hand on her heart. Another series of scampers brought the rabbit within her reach. He sat up on his hind legs and regarded her with a wrinkling nose and shivering whiskers. One of his ears was white on the tip, like it had been dipped in paint. He startled her by suddenly dashing forward and pouncing on her feet. Then, just as quickly, he returned to his earlier spot a few steps away.

Odd behavior for certain, Samantha thought, before the rabbit came closer and jumped at her feet again. This bunny baffled Sam, until she noticed something. The rabbit jumped at her feet repeatedly, each time retreating a few steps farther away. It was almost as if he was beckoning her to get up off the log and go for a hop.

"Well," thought Sam, "I'm not going to pass up the chance to play tag with a rabbit." She took a break from her wallowing and followed him. A few timid steps, and then she stopped. He charged at her again before sprinting away toward a pile of leaves several yards away. The rabbit ran around the pile once and stopped in front of it, staring at her.

Sam thought it was strange to see that pile here. Who would have created such a thing in this clearing? The rabbit hopped around it again, which was even more perplexing. Sam stepped closer with curiosity, and addressed the rabbit.

"I wish you could talk!" She muttered. "Then you could explain a few things to me, like why—" Her question was interrupted by a peculiar sound. A tiny moan coming from the leaf pile?

Sam's heart skipped a beat as she fell to her knees next to the leaves. She brought her face close to the middle of it.

"Tara?" she whispered. A whimper emerged,

and although it sounded miserable, Sam sobbed in relief. Slowly and carefully, she lifted one leaf at time off the top, until Tara's small, dozing figure was visible.

"Tara!" Sam gulped softly. The young Woodlander blinked several times and looked up at Sam through bloodshot eyes.

"Sam?" Tara tried to sit up but winced in pain. Tears streamed down her dirty face as Samantha cleared away the leaves around her.

"It's going to be okay, Tara," Sam assured her. "I'll get you back to the homestead so that Elsa can take care of you. Everyone there is very worried about you. How did you end up here?"

Tara looked around thoughtfully but did not answer.

Samantha tried to appear calm, but this was difficult. She could see that Tara's arm was bent at a freakish angle, obviously broken. It would be a challenge to get her home.

"I think I busted my arm," Tara said in a puzzled tone. "I can't remember, I must have fallen, or ..." Before she could say more, her face crumpled into a wrinkled mess of tears.

Putting aside her own curiosity, Sam patiently comforted her.

"Don't try to talk anymore, Tara. I think we should make a sling for your arm so it won't hurt so much. Then I'll carry you as carefully as I can." Her mind raced ahead, devising some sort of support for Tara's broken limb. Remembering a hair ribbon in her backpack, she hoped that would do.

"Are you hurt anywhere else?" she asked, relieved to see Tara shake her head slowly in response.

"My ankle hurts a little, but not as bad as my arm," Tara sniffled. "And both my shoulders are bleeding."

"It'll be okay," Sam reassured her. Unfastening the strap around her waist, she brought her pack onto her lap and began foraging for the ribbon.

A rustling sound nearby startled Sam, but she was unafraid. Turning around, her gaze settled on exactly what she was looking for: the friendly face of Tara's guardian rabbit. The white tip of his ear flopped forward. He acknowledged Sam's bow of gratitude with a satisfied sneeze before nimbly returning to the safety of the bushes.

"Tara, have you ever seen a rabbit smile?" asked Sam.

A bit bewildered, but happy for the distraction, Tara replied with certainty, "Lots of times."

Sam splinted Tara's arm as best she could, and wrapped her gently in her blue scarf. She tried to distract Tara from the pain by telling her all about the rabbit. She told a very colorful story, although it didn't need much to make it remarkable.

* ★ ★

Tom headed back to the homestead alone, with a heavy heart. Palmer had gone home. Tom dreaded telling Marta and the others that the search was unsuccessful. His plan was to check in and head back out immediately in another direction.

Weariness and frustration dulled his senses as he approached the beech tree. He thought he heard a lullaby nearby, the humming of a sweet melody. He turned, raising his tired head in curiosity. It was Sam, stepping softly and singing, with a small bundle in her arms.

She looked happy to spot him there on the trail, so he felt that Tara must be okay. He ran to meet her halfway. She knelt down carefully in front of him.

"Tara's arm is broken, Tom, but otherwise she seems fine," she assured him. He let out the long breath he had been holding, and with it, his shoulders relaxed.

"She's asleep," Sam continued. "I think she might have hit her head because she can't remember much. That happened to my little brother once and he was fine the next day," she whispered. She placed Tara into Tom's outstretched arms, tucking in the edges of her scarf that she had used for a blanket.

"Elsa will take care of her," Tom said between

tears. "If you will open the door for me, I can manage to carry her down the stairs."

Sam crawled toward the roots where the door was hidden. Reaching inside, she lifted the tiny bolt and pushed open the double doors. Making room then for Tom, she sat back on her heels.

"Samantha, we can't thank you enough for what you have done today," declared Tom. "Please get home safely now. Come by tomorrow, if you can, to check on Tara and tell us all the details. We will look forward to seeing you then." With an affectionate half-smile in her direction, Tom disappeared beneath the roots, holding Tara close. Samantha bent down and reached in to close the double doors behind him.

★　★　★

Rising up to stand, Sam stretched her limbs. She was hungry and cold, but felt peaceful. It had been several hours since she had ventured out, and she knew that her parents would be watching for her return. Knowing that she could do nothing else for Tara at this point, Sam let go of any worry she was bearing. Even in her tiredness, a warm energy filled her body that shortened the distance home.

Approaching her yard, Samantha could hear Jared laughing. She glimpsed him on the patio with their Grandpa Jack, carving pumpkins. In all the drama with Tara, Sam had completely forgotten that it was Halloween.

Sam's exhaustion faded as she thought of her costume and the upcoming party at Lulu's house. The MacKenzies went crazy over Halloween. Lulu's older brother and sister, Cara and Cody, turned the yard into a haunted graveyard, and all their high school friends came over to scare the trick-or-treaters. Cara and Cody took care of the youngest kids, making sure they all had fun and weren't too frightened. Lulu's Grandpa Martin always dressed up as a vampire, and handed out the candy.

"There you are!" hollered Grandpa Jack across the yard. Sam yawned as she joined them on the patio.

Jared eyed his sister with a frown. "I hope you aren't too tired to carve punkins," he said, plopping a big scoop of seeds onto some newspaper.

"No way, Jared," she assured him. "I'm going to make mine look like it's laughing, since yours is so scary."

Jared smiled, and regarded his efforts. They finished the jack-o'-lanterns and carried them around to the front steps. Jared ran inside to put on his cowboy costume, and Grandpa Jack followed him. Sam sat down on the steps next to the pumpkins to wait for her friends.

Palmer, Samantha and Lulu were dressing up as their favorite foods. Sam's Belgian waffle costume was simple enough. She had painted a long tee shirt to look like a waffle, and tied a black, yellow and red scarf around her neck. She wore a little jar of maple syrup as a necklace, and a pat of butter made out of felt on her head. Lulu was going as French toast, and Palmer as a crescent roll. They had planned to meet at Sam's before heading over to Lulu's for early dinner and trick-or-treating.

Lulu appeared around the corner carrying a shopping bag. "Hey, Sam," she hollered. "Where's Palmer?"

"Hi," Sam smiled in Lulu's direction. "He's not here yet."

Palmer snuck up on them as they removed Lulu's costume from the bag. He jumped out from behind the bushes and landed at their feet, trying to scare them. A giant crescent roll wasn't very frightening, so they laughed at his failed attempts. The three of them got ready and headed over to Lulu's.

As the afternoon turned into evening, it grew colder. Sam was glad she had worn a sweatshirt under her costume. The MacKenzies' yard looked amazing. Dozens of fake tombstones with silly names on them covered the lawn. The house was lit with creepy green and yellow lights. The smell of grilled hot dogs filled the chilly air. Martin stood at the open front door in his vampire costume, breathing heavily next to the candy bowl. Lulu's parents sat on a bench dressed as Frankenstein and his bride. They laughed and talked with Sam's parents, who were perfect as peanut butter and jelly.

Biting into a hot dog, Sam watched Cara and Cody. They were four years older than Lulu. Dressed as zombies, they staggered around the yard, grumbling and groaning. The neighborhood kids knew it was them and kept coming back for more.

Sam remembered a few years ago when the twins had been at the Lamp Lighting and the fun she and Palmer had had with them. Cara and Cody were both Protectlings. She recalled that they hadn't been at the last two Lamp Lightings, or the Butternut Harvests.

Her hot dog had grown cold in her hand as she wondered about their absence. Sam's eyes followed the twins as they stumbled around the tombstones. Later, she noticed that Cara and Cody stayed behind as the kids all headed out to go trick-or-treating. She watched them remove their costumes and go into the house with their friends to watch a movie.

The front door of Lulu's house closed, and the yard darkened. Sam grabbed her empty pillowcase and ran to join her friends.

NOVEMBER

Sam went to Lulu's in the morning to help clean up the yard and take down the Halloween decorations. She walked up the path, checking out the cardboard tombstones and fake spider webs. She rang the doorbell and bent to pick up a snickers wrapper off the steps. Puffs of her frosty breath hung around her face for a fleeting moment before vanishing.

Lulu's grandpa answered the door. "Morning, Samantha," Martin smiled.

"How are you, Mr. MacKenzie?" Sam greeted him.

"Lulu and the kids are just finishing up breakfast. I'm meeting your grandfather in a few minutes to plan the spring fundraiser for the Rawlings Conservation Fund. Cara and Cody are helping out for their service project. They've taken such an interest lately!" he added. The two of them headed back to the kitchen.

"I'd love to help, too," added Sam. "Just let me know what needs to be done. You know how much I love those woods."

Martin looked at her with interest. "There's plenty to do, Sam. I know you're quite the artist— perhaps you can make some posters and flyers? Let me get back to you with some action items after the meeting."

Sam nodded with a smile. She thanked him and took off her coat, joining the noisy group at the breakfast table. Even though she had just eaten breakfast, she had some pumpkin pancakes and bacon. Then the gang spent a few hours getting the place back to order.

Over the next few weeks, Sam worked on some sketches for eight posters to put up at the middle school. One was a drawing of the giant beech tree with the words 'Preserve, Conserve, and Protect' surrounding it, and the details of the Fun Fair which would be held at the high school to raise money. Jack and Martin liked it so much that they asked Sam if they could use it on all the stationery and website for the Rawlings Conservation Fund. They were planning to sell tee shirts printed with it as well. Sam planned to tell the Woodlanders all about it when she checked in on Tara.

Sam had been to visit Tara once, but couldn't see her in the Infirmary. That room was far beneath the tree where a Protectling couldn't go. Marta and Tom filled Sam in on Tara's progress and brought Tara news and well wishes from Sam as well.

★　★　★

Thanksgiving Day was clear and sunny. Leaves blew around the yard as Samantha's grandparents drove up and parked in the driveway. Aunt Beth and Uncle Paul pushed the babies in the stroller down Primrose Lane. Jared welcomed everyone, running circles around them.

The Penning home was filled with delicious smells and chattering loved ones. Jared showed Grandpa Jack and Gram Ellen his latest construction projects. Paige and Oliver were passed around from one set of arms to another, wide-eyed and wary. Everyone helped out in the kitchen, filling platters and mashing potatoes.

"Turkey time!" Sam's dad called, rubbing his hands together. Everyone made their way into the dining room, where a beautiful table was set. Jared had made place mats for each person, their names colored brightly on construction paper.

"Do I get to take mine home, I hope? It's going right on the refrigerator," Grandpa Jack promised, after Jared gave him permission.

Sam had contributed the centerpiece: a turkey made out of a pineapple, wisteria pods as tail feathers, and a lemon for a head. His wattle was a red Swedish fish candy secured with a toothpick.

"Wow, Sam. You're a clever sculptor!" Gram Ellen commented. "He's gorgeous."

Sam looked at her creation. Every year she made 'Tom For The Table', but for the first time he just looked silly to her.

"I think Jared will do a much better job next year," Sam promised. He lit up at this, and climbed up on the table to study the centerpiece up close, from all angles. Her grandfather brought the real turkey to the table then, and everyone sat down for the feast.

The babies cried through most of the meal, but settled down a bit while the table was cleared and pumpkin and pecan pies were served.

"I think the twins would fall asleep if we took them for a little walk," said Aunt Beth. "Let's bundle up and head outside for some fresh air."

"Great idea," Sam's mom agreed. "Let's head into the woods." Everyone brightened up at this proposition. Everyone, except Sam.

"No, not the woods. Let's stick to the neighborhood," she blurted. Jared shook his head.

"I want to play in the leaves!" he shouted. Beth smiled patiently.

"The woods are more exciting than the sidewalk, Sam. Get your coats! It's not too cold today, and the sun'll be shining for a few more hours."

"I'll lead the way," Sam offered, eager to keep her family away from the beech tree.

"Great!" her dad added. "Sam knows her way

around back there. She can show us where all the fairies live," he said earnestly to Jared. Her brother gasped and raced off to find his coat.

★　★　★

Next to a warm fire in the homestead, Tara napped peacefully. It had been almost a month since her accident. Elsa had reset her badly broken arm and wrapped it from elbow to wrist in linen strips dipped in a paste made from limestone powder mixed with water. It had dried hard and heavy, so Elsa refashioned the yellow ribbon sling. Tara also had a broken rib and a sprained ankle and puncture wounds on her shoulders.

Elsa sat by her side in a willow rocker, using a mortar and pestle to grind dried yellow arnica flowers into a paste for bruises. Tara's were faded now, but she had been covered in them, from head to toe. Her cast could come off next week, but she still had frequent headaches, and got dizzy when she sat up. She had no memory of what had happened to her.

Marta and Tom rested at the foot of the bed. For several weeks now they had filled the days reading and repairing holes in winter socks, knitting caps and vests. Many hours of this had left them fidgety and bored, but they would not leave Tara's side. Tom stood, stretching with a loud, lion-like yawn.

"Hush!" whispered Elsa. "You'll wake her. Her broken bones will heal faster if she can sleep deeply." Tom sat back down sheepishly, addressing Marta quietly.

"I really need some fresh air," he whispered. "How about a climb to The Outlook? We won't be gone long, and a little exercise will do us both good," he suggested. He knew the treetop observatory was one of Marta's favorite spots, but she shook her head. It was one of Tara's favorites as well, but she wouldn't be able to make the climb.

Elsa leaned toward her. "Really, Marta. You need to get out for a bit. I'll be right here. Tara would want you to feel the sun on your face, don't you think?" The three of them looked at Tara. A brief, dreamy smile played across her mouth, offering Marta the permission she needed.

"Alright, but only for a bit. If she wakes up, tell her we are coming right back," Marta instructed Elsa.

"Of course, Dear. You just gave her some soup a half hour ago. She knows you have been here the whole time. Go," Elsa kissed Marta on her cheek and pushed her toward the door. Tom hugged his mother-in-law before following Marta. They both stopped, reluctant to leave.

"Go!" Elsa mouthed silently, shooing them away.

★　★　★

Jared was the first one to reach the gate into the woods, but he wasn't tall enough to open it by himself. He jumped repeatedly at the latch before racing back to the group in the yard. Running circles around them made the babies laugh, but it also seemed to slow the progress toward the woods, so he tried yelling instead.

"Hurry up!" he pleaded. "Do the fairies have Thanksgiving? Maybe we'll see them celebrating!" He looked so happily excited that Sam hated to dash his hopes.

"There are no fairies, Jared," she told him. "Just squirrels and chipmunks. No winged, tiny people flying around."

"NO," Jared declared. "I saw tiny footprints in our yard, in the mud. I know they live out here. Dad says so," he added, looking to him for support. His father was deep in conversation with Paul and didn't hear them.

Sam opened the gate, and she and Jared proceeded into the woods ahead of the others. Her plan to direct everyone toward the creek was thwarted as Jared took off running in the opposite direction.

"Yikes, Jared. We're going the other way!" she hollered after him, but he didn't respond.

"Please go after him, Sam," her mom yelled

from behind. "We'll catch up."

Samantha sighed and rolled her eyes. The beech tree was far enough away from the trail. Still, having her entire family in the woods, headed in the general direction of the homestead, made her uncomfortable. She was nervously burping up pumpkin pie and stuffing.

"Jared, wait up!" she shouted, suddenly calmer with a plan. "I think I see a fairy trail over here!" Lying didn't come naturally to her, and she squirmed under the discomfort of it. The sound of Jared's galloping footsteps came closer and he crashed into her, out of breath. They both tumbled to the ground in a heap.

There was a horrible crunching noise, followed by Sam's cry of pain. She gasped for breath and clutched at her ankle, fighting back tears. Jared stood quickly.

"What's wrong, Sam?" His eyes were wide and his lip was trembling. "Are you okay? I'm sorry I knocked you over!" He was crying now, seeing his sister on the ground. He'd landed on her ankle with the force of a charging bull.

"I'm fine," she assured him, although her tone was not convincing.

He shook his head. "No, you're not fine," he mumbled, as he ran off toward the sound of his parents' voices close by on the trail. "Mom! Sam's hurt!" She heard him repeating this, over and over.

She winced in pain.

Within a few seconds, her grandfather was by her side. "Where does it hurt, Sam?" he asked, gently.

"My ankle," she showed him, rolling up her pant leg. It was already swollen and turning a ghastly purple. The rest of the family formed a circle around her. Her mother knelt down next to her grandfather, and Sam leaned against her.

"It looks broken," she concluded, smoothing Sam's hair out of her face. "Don't worry, Hun. We'll take care of you."

"Let's get you home," her dad declared with concern. Her grandmother and aunt fretted as her Grandpa Jack lifted her off the ground. He was a big man, but gentle as a lamb. The pain in her ankle was excruciating, causing her to sob into her grandfather's chest. Poor Jared was so upset by her tears that he cried along with her.

★   ★   ★

In the tallest boughs of the beech tree, Marta and Tom stood upon the oak platform built by Walter many years ago. The Outlook was a miniature treehouse—one square room with walls halfway up, and no ceiling. A dangerous climb on pegs nailed into the tree trunk led to a trap door in the floor.

Walter maintained it regularly, making sure it

was a safe spot for his favorite hobby: stargazing. It was sturdy, but Tom still felt dizzy up so high with expansive views of the treetops in every direction. With the leaves down, the woods took on a brown, stark appearance. The sound of the wind this time of year was also different. Without the rustling of green foliage, it rattled the empty branches. The far-off creek sounded as if it were trickling right under them.

"It really does clear my mind being up here," Tom remarked, gulping a large breath of air and exhaling it slowly. They were bundled cozily in felt coats, wool mittens and knitted caps. "I hope you can relax a bit and let go of worrying about Tara. She is mostly healed, and she is going to be just fine," he promised, placing his hand on Marta's shoulder.

"Yes, the fresh air and sunshine do help a bit," she agreed. Closing her eyes and facing the sun, she soaked up the rays with a sigh.

Just then, a nearby cry of distress disturbed the peaceful moment. "Someone is hurt," Marta said. They both shuffled to the corner of the lookout and faced toward the sound.

"Can you see anything?" she asked Tom, craning her neck.

"No. There are more voices, though. It's a group of Dumans." This compounded their worry. "Sounds like they are on the trail. No need to be alarmed," he assured her.

Marta tilted her head. "I think it is Sam," she reflected with concern. "Her face is clear to me in my mind right now," she added, rubbing at her heart with her right hand.

"I sense that as well," Tom nodded.

They knew what to do. Removing their mittens, they clasped hands and closed their eyes. Silently wishing comfort and peace for Samantha, warmth spread over them and radiated outward. They imagined its glow being carried off by the wind, blowing downward in the direction of the voices they had heard below.

Opening their eyes, Marta and Tom observed the peaceful state filling their quiet perch. They smiled at one another.

"It will be all right," Tom concluded. Marta sighed and gave him a small smile. They put on their mittens and headed toward the trap door, eager to check in on Tara.

★   ★   ★

Halfway home, securely cradled in her grandfather's arms, Samantha was trying to think of anything but the pain. She was eager but unable to comfort her little brother.

"Sam will be just fine, Jared," his mother lovingly assured him. "It was an accident, Sweetie. Let's make her a get-well card when we get home, okay?" she offered.

He sniffled at this. "A big one," he nodded. "She can have more pie, too. As much as she wants."

The wind picked up then, swirling the leaves around them. It was a warm gust, blasting the cold air away from Sam's exposed ankle.

"How odd," commented her grandfather. He held her close. "Seems to be a mild breeze following us home. Downright balmy," he added.

Sam closed her eyes and absorbed the warmth. Along with her grandfather's heartbeat, it lessened her pain and comforted her greatly.

DECEMBER

Tara sat in the Infirmary, warming herself by the fire. She was better now, sleeping in her own bed at night back in the family quarters. Elsa had removed her cast that morning, and had fashioned a sling in its place.

"I hope Samantha will come visit soon, since I can get to the Great Hall now to visit with her," Tara remarked to Elsa. Her grandmother was at her worktable, pouring boiling water over a mixture of dried horsetail grass and comfrey leaves. The tea smelled like a dirty dishrag.

"I think it will be a while, Dear," Elsa answered. "Your parents believe that she is recovering from an injury. We just have to be patient," she added, bringing the steaming mug over to her granddaughter.

Tara crinkled her nose at it. "Ugh! I can't drink this anymore!" She pushed the mug away and covered her nose and mouth with her free hand. "It smells gross, and tastes like dirt," she complained with a scowl.

"I'll put some honey in it for you, but you have to drink it to strengthen your bones," Elsa insisted. "How are your shoulders feeling?" she asked, reaching to check the bandages. Under them was the biggest injury, mostly healed by now: large, deep puncture wounds, front and back. They were obviously not from thorns. Elsa shuddered to think about the hungry hawk that probably tried to feed Tara to its young. Somehow, she had escaped, and Elsa was grateful. She patted her granddaughter's cheek tenderly.

The large bump on Tara's head had diminished. Her bruises and cuts had faded away, aided by Elsa's rubs and ointments.

Tara tried a strained shrug. "They're tight and achy," she answered. "I hope Sam has someone like you taking care of her."

"Her mother is a doctor," Elsa replied. "I'm sure she has plenty of stinky tea to drink." Tara made a horrified face, and they both laughed. Their giggles subsided and were replaced by quiet sighs. Tara's expression became serious.

"This is her last winter as a Protectling, isn't it?" she asked. "What if she is healing at home all of December and we don't get to see her?"

The question hung heavily between them. "Winter would be hard without her, but there are other Protectlings to help us," Elsa reminded Tara. "We'll see her soon," Elsa promised, securing a soft blanket around her shoulders. They both turned to the fire in sorrow.

Tara stared at the flames. "I think Samantha is different from the rest of the Dumans," she reflected, forcing down a gulp of tea. "I know that she could always be a Protectling." She blinked at her grandmother as she sat down next to the hearth.

Elsa reached over and took Tara's hand in her own. "I know she is a special friend to you. The two of you share a strong bond, but she is not different. Already she is showing signs of their mindset. That's what happens at her age. Her world is expanding beyond these woods, as it should. But with that, she might learn things that are not true."

Tara shook her head in disagreement. "I don't understand. When we grow up, we don't unlearn what is true. Why do they?"

"They do not unlearn it as much as they seem to cover it up with other things," she said. "It becomes buried."

Tara could not follow what her grandmother was saying. "What do you mean by their mindset?" she asked.

Elsa tried to explain. "We are all born knowing the truth: that every living thing is connected to all living things. Dumans and Woodlanders, animals, trees, wildflowers ... The link is strong, running like a river and burning like a fire. We can use the link to thrive and take care of one other. Everything we need is all around us. Do you understand this?" she paused, waiting for a sign from Tara.

"Yes, I see," Tara replied.

Elsa continued, "Dumans do not see. They want more. It is not enough for them. They are willing to harm one living thing to have more for themselves. Once that choice has been made, it can become a pattern. Then it is their mindset."

Tara was beginning to understand, but something didn't make sense to her.

"Samantha would never harm us, or any living thing, no matter what," she stated with certainty. Elsa agreed.

"Of course, Sam has a good heart and always will. However, she is absorbing Duman beliefs as she is growing. She may become separated from the truth." Elsa folded her hands in her lap. "The things Sam has learned from being a Protectling will stay within her heart, no matter what," she assured Tara. "The rest is up to her, and she must be left in freedom to choose her own life."

Looking into her mug, Tara watched a tear drop into the brown liquid. She placed it onto the hearth, half finished and cold. Elsa didn't scold her, but got up to make a pot of sweet tea for them to share.

★　★　★

Samantha sat in the window seat after school,

drinking hot chocolate. Her ankle was broken. She sported a neon orange cast, decorated with signatures in every color from her classmates. It covered her heel and extended up to her knee. Even Maddie had written 'get well soon' in purple. Sam admired Jared's portrait of Bunny on the top of her foot.

Lumbering around school on crutches left her exhausted. Worse than that was being stuck at home every afternoon. She hadn't been able to get back to the homestead to check on Tara. Her parents wouldn't allow her to venture into the woods until her cast came off.

She'd received a kind message from Marta and Tom, wishing her well and instructing her to stay put until she was better. It wasn't a surprise to her that they were aware of her broken ankle. They knew about everything that happened at Woods Edge.

A big winter storm was on its way. It was all over the news on TV and the radio. Eighteen to twenty inches of snow were expected, which troubled Sam. The Woodlanders' stovepipes and chimneys would need to be cleared after the storm. Doorways under old trees would need to be unblocked. It had taken her a few seasons to become good at these jobs. She worried that another Protectling might not know how to do them.

A perfect chance presented itself for her to sneak out to the homestead that afternoon. Her mother would be leaving soon to take Jared to his karate lesson. They'd be gone for two hours; plenty of time for her to see how Tara was doing. She was eager to let the Woodlanders know about the coming storm and show them that she could complete her regular jobs just fine on crutches. Sam convinced herself that this was a good plan. She ignored a twinge of doubt and hobbled over to the kitchen table to finish her homework.

Sam tried to focus on the fractions in her math book. A nagging discomfort distracted her. Unplanned visits to the homestead were not allowed—every Protectling knew this. Samantha told herself that this was a special case. She was certain that she knew better and could bend the rules.

Her mom leaned in from the doorway. "Will you be all right here on your own for a bit, Sam? Palmer's mother is home if you need anything," she added.

"I'll be fine, Mom. I have lots of homework." Sam held both her palms up over the stacks of books on the table. "I'll be sitting right here when you get back," she smiled. Her mom nodded, and headed for the garage with Jared in tow.

Samantha looked out the window. The sky was gray and looked darker than usual for the afternoon.

She figured she had two hours until her mother and Jared got home—plenty of time to get to the homestead and back before dinner. Standing up, she reached for her crutches. Her underarms were sore, and her ankle was throbbing. Struggling into her coat left her sweating. She sat back down at the kitchen table, laid her head on her forearms, and started to cry.

There was a tapping at the sliding patio door. Samantha raised her head and blinked away her tears. She couldn't see anyone there, but her eyes were a little blurry. The tapping continued, and she lowered her gaze to see Walter, knocking on the glass. She made her way there as fast as she could on her crutches. Opening the door an inch, she let Walter in along with a burst of cold air.

"Brrrr!" he exclaimed, stepping in and rubbing his mittened hands on his arms. He wore a hooded wool coat and tall boots. Sam was delighted to see him. It was unusual for him to be out at Woods Edge in the daylight, and she wondered why he had made the trip. She looked out into the yard and saw Palmer leaving, heading toward his house.

Walter looked up at her in her coat. "Are you going somewhere, Sam? I waited for your mom and brother to leave so that I could visit with you. I hope you are not on your way out?"

Sam forgot she had her coat on. "No, I was just cold," she sniffed. She wiped her nose with her sleeve. She thought she must look very tired and perhaps sick, with red eyes and a runny nose. Smiling as best she could, she welcomed him into the warm room.

"Please come in and sit," she said, quietly. "It's so great to see you!" She leaned her crutches against the wall and sat down in the window seat, carefully propping up her ankle on a cushion. Walter removed his coat and boots. Sam reached down and gently lifted him up beside her. He sat back against a pillow and sank comfortably into it.

"Such a soft place to rest!" He smiled over at her. "I hope you are recovering well," he added. "We have all been thinking of you every day, wishing you speedy healing." Samantha nodded and thanked him.

"How's Tara?" asked Sam. "I've been thinking of her every day, too." Walter assured her that Tara was better.

"She sends her love," he added. Walter looked out the window. "Palmer will be back for me soon. He has headed home to fetch some old wool sweaters out of the Goodwill basket for us to make winter blankets. I was eager to have the chance to check in on you in the meantime."

This made her forget all about her throbbing foot. She was so happy to see Walter and hear good news about Tara.

"I was worried about the storm that's coming,"

Samantha told him. "It's going to be a big one." Walter nodded.

"I love the big storms!" he told her. "So cozy in the homestead. Nothing as hushed as the day after a storm under the beech tree. It's toasty warm by the fire, and we have plenty of food, water, and firewood. You don't need to worry." He moved closer and patted her hand.

Samantha remembered something. "I can come out after it's over and clear the stovepipes and chimneys for you—" Walter interrupted her.

"Absolutely not!" He looked horrified. "Out in two feet of snow on crutches? Don't even consider it. Palmer has taught the younger Protectlings from Wisteria Street how to clear the chimneys for us, so it will be taken care of. There won't be any duties for you until spring, my dear. You must heal. That is the most important thing," he assured her.

Sam felt much better. She wondered why she had ever considered going out in the cold, risking getting hurt again. She realized that she had been thinking about herself, not the Woodlanders. They were going to be fine. She could let go.

Walter could tell by the look on Samantha's face that his visit had been worthwhile. She looked calm and happy. He would tell Tara this, and it would do her good.

Palmer returned then, tapping on the glass door. He held up a shopping bag filled with sweaters.

"I'm off then!" Walter smiled at Sam. "So good to see you, my dear."

Sam helped him down from the window seat and waved at Palmer. She watched the two of them head into the woods.

That night the storm hit hard. The Woodlanders were safe in the homestead, drinking hot cider by their fires. Samantha slept well. She dreamed of running fast, free of her cast and crutches.

The next day, the snow lay deep in drifts against the houses. School was cancelled, and the power was out in most of the neighborhood. Smoke billowed out of all the chimneys, as fires burned to warm the dark homes.

After a day of reading and playing Battleship, Samantha and her family gathered around the fireplace in the family room. Her dad had shoveled a path out to the grill to cook a chicken. Her mom wrapped potatoes in foil and made some brownies in an old tin tray on the grill as well. The brownies tasted a little smoky, but were delicious—crunchy on the outside and gooey in the middle. They ate at the table with candles burning. After dinner, their dad read aloud from *Treasure Island*. They all fell asleep together in a heap of blankets and pillows in front of the fire. Samantha wished that the power would go out more often.

In the morning, the power was back on, but school was still cancelled. All the kids were out sledding down Rawlings Knoll, but Samantha was stuck inside. She tried to enjoy some quiet time up in her room sketching, but she could hear their hollering and laughter outside her window. The noise distracted her. She scowled at her crutches, propped against her desk.

Her mom came into her room carrying a plate of leftover brownies.

"There's someone here to see you," she announced, blocking Sam's view of whoever it was. When her mother bent down to leave the plate on the desk, Maddie appeared from behind her. Her nose was red and her hair was damp with melting snow.

"Hey," Maddie waved, plopping herself down on Sam's bed.

"Hey," Sam replied, not sure what else to say. She wondered why Maddie would choose to come see her rather than play in the snow with the other kids. Even Palmer and Lulu weren't visiting today.

Her mom looked from Maddie to Sam. Conversation failed to begin, so she spoke up.

"Well, why don't you two have some brownies. I'm going to check on Jared in the back yard." Her mom grabbed one for herself off the plate, blinked wide-eyed at Sam, and ducked out of the room.

Maddie took a brownie and bit into it. "This is delicious," she said, licking her lips. "It tastes like s'mores," she added, popping the rest in her mouth.

"We baked them on the grill," Sam told her. She faced her chair toward the bed where Maddie was sitting. They both smiled and took another brownie off the plate.

"What are you working on?" Maddie pointed to the sketchbook lying open on the desk. Sam wondered if Maddie would tease her about her drawings. She wasn't eager to show them to her. She turned around and picked up the sketchbook, planning to close it and put it in the drawer.

At the last second, she changed her mind and brought it over to Maddie, open to the drawing she had been working on. It was a sketch of Jared's snowmen that she could see out her window. They were actually three large snow bunnies, sitting upright, facing one another in a circle. Samantha was impressed by his work, and thought it might please Jared to have a record of his sculptures. She hadn't planned on showing anyone else.

Maddie grabbed the sketchbook. "I love to draw," she told Sam. "I have fourteen full sketchbooks, but I never show them to anyone," confessed Maddie.

Sam was surprised to hear this. She felt a new connection to this girl who didn't seem to like anything. Sam realized that she had spent so much time avoiding Maddie, she hadn't gotten to know her very well yet.

Maddie stood up with the sketchbook and headed over to the window, looking down into the yard and back at the drawing a few times. "Wow," she said. "This is amazing. You're a great artist," she added, sitting back down on the bed. Sam thanked her and reached for it, but Maddie held tight.

"Can I look at the rest?" she asked Sam. There were a few drawings in there of the Woodlanders, so Samantha hesitated. Maddie didn't notice, and began flipping through the front of the book. She stopped at a picture of the beech tree for a moment, and then stared at a few others before stopping at another and squinting at it. It was a drawing of the Woodlanders in a circle at the Lantern Lighting.

"Be the Light," Maddie read aloud in a singsong voice, giggling. Nervousness bubbled up in Sam's belly, but she didn't sense any nastiness in Maddie's laughter.

"I like this one best," Maddie said, pointing at the Woodlanders. "They look really happy," she sighed. Sam relaxed when it didn't seem like Maddie wanted to ask any questions about the drawing of the amber token, or the one she had done of the Great Hall.

"You make stuff up a lot, huh?" Maddie commented, stopping at a colored pencil drawing of the braided ladder.

Samantha shrugged. "I have a big imagination," she admitted.

"Me too," Maddie told her. "I'm weird, just like you," she said, without looking up from the sketchbook. "I want to be an artist when I grow up, or maybe a movie director or producer. What do you want to be?"

So Maddie thinks weird is a good thing, Sam thought, before answering. "I want to start a school that teaches people how to be happy," Sam told her.

Maddie nodded. "That's a weird idea," she said, with seriousness. "There are no schools like that. Let's draw some pictures of what it might look like."

Maddie jumped off the bed and got the jar of colored pencils off the desk. There was a pack of new sketchbooks from her grandmother in the drawer, so Sam went to her desk and took them out, handing one to Maddie. Her eyes lit up as she took it from Sam.

The afternoon passed quickly. Sam and Maddie designed school buildings, floor plans, playgrounds and gardens. They worked on a list of books that everyone should read, and a list of classes that should be taught, like How To Draw, How To Listen, How to Work, How To Play, and How To Help.

Maddie looked out the window and noticed

that it was getting dark. "I have to go home now," she told Sam. "I'll leave this here so we can work on it next time." She handed the sketchbook to Samantha and jumped down from the bed, stretching her arms above her head and yawning loudly. Sam thanked Maddie, and listened to her bound down the stairs.

Looking through their drawings, Sam admired Maddie's ideas for the school. Maddie was a really good artist. She drew quickly, with big lines and lots of color. Her handwriting was messy, but kind of pretty.

JANUARY

The rest of the winter wasn't as bad as Sam thought it would be, stuck inside with her cast. Palmer and Lulu spent a few afternoons with her, but mostly they went sledding. Maddie came over often, and the two of them filled many sketchbooks. They worked on plans for The Happiness School, and wrote two screenplays for movies that Maddie planned to direct. During the week, Palmer, Lulu, Samantha and Maddie ate lunch together in the middle school cafeteria.

Finally it was time to get her cast removed. After coming home from the doctor's office, she begged her mom to let her have some time alone in the woods.

"Okay," her mother told her. "Dress warmly and wear your boots. And be home before dark!" She shouted after her as Sam raced out the back door.

Sam's ankle felt itchy in her boot as her footsteps crunched on the snow. She focused on the sound of it and the feel of the crisp, cold air against her face. She breathed it in huge gulps. Last night Sam had received a message from Marta and Tom requesting her help at the water well, if she was able. It had been a long time since she had seen the Woodlanders, and she missed them.

Tara and Palmer greeted her as she came into the clearing.

"Samantha!" Tara hollered. "It's so good to see you on your feet," she added. She was wearing a long wool coat with a pack on her back, and matching hat and mittens. Palmer was damp in his coat and snow pants from sledding. The three of them started walking to the well, which wasn't far from the beech tree.

"It's good to see you all better, too," Sam said. "How's your arm?" she asked, pointing to Tara's sling. Sam's yellow ribbon was a bit worse for wear, but had been put to good use.

"Better," Tara replied. She told them that she had to wear a sling until her muscles got stronger. Her shoulders were damaged, and she still couldn't remember what had happened that day.

"I can't lift my arms over my head, but that's okay. I will be able to after I do more of my exercises. Elsa is taking very good care of me," she smiled.

They reached the spot where the well was hidden. A huge granite boulder rose up from the snow, several feet taller than Palmer and Samantha.

It was rounded at its front, and flat like a wall on its other side. Palmer picked up Tara and placed her gently on a small ledge in the middle, where she settled down on her pack. Sam and Palmer started to clear away the snow close to the flat side, revealing a large rock that covered the well. Together, they lifted it and propped it up against the boulder.

Tara informed them that the water had a bad smell, so the Woodlanders couldn't drink it. They hoped that Sam and Palmer could take a look and figure out what was wrong. When they moved aside the cover, stinky fumes had escaped.

"Yuck," Palmer said, turning away from the well.

Sam crinkled her nose. "It's not that bad," she told them, peering into the dark hole. She couldn't see the bottom. The water was below the freeze line, so there wouldn't be any ice down there. She grabbed a small handful of snow and formed it into a ball, then dropped it down the well. A moment passed before they heard it plunk into the water below.

"I think a burrowing animal must have dug through, fallen in and drowned. We'll have to fish it out," Palmer added.

Tara whined. "Poor thing. I hope it's not a rabbit. Good thing it's cold or it would be much stinkier!" Last summer they had found a dead groundhog in the well. "We had to get water from the stream for a whole month until the smell cleared last August. It was so gross," she recalled, turning away with a scowl.

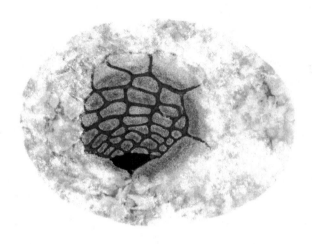

Palmer had been the one to fish out the dead groundhog, so he knew what to do. He had come prepared with some yarn from his sister's knitting box and a colander from the kitchen. He reached into his backpack and handed them over to Sam.

She set to work tying them together. Palmer also brought a flashlight, which really helped. Sam held it with the beam shining into the well so that Palmer could get at whatever was floating on the surface of the water down there. They could see some dark object bobbing around, and Sam shined the light on it.

Several times Palmer lowered the colander and

swished it around. He couldn't seem to get the floating shape. It disappeared beneath the water.

"It's sinking," Sam told him. "We'll never get it if it goes to the bottom," she told him. "You can do it. Focus your thoughts and take your time," she told him gently.

Palmer took a deep breath and tried again. "Got it!" He exhaled, and brought it up carefully, slowly, hand over hand. The metal colander banged against the stone of the well, but he held on.

When the strainer became visible, Sam reached in and grabbed it. Her heart sank when she saw the animal in it: a brown rabbit, with one white-tipped ear. He was limp and waterlogged, and smelled terrible. Sam didn't care about the foul odor. She brought the dripping colander onto her lap and held it tight. A sob bubbled up from her throat and tears spilled over her cheeks. She sat back heavily in the snow.

Tara sighed from her perch on the boulder. "It's him, isn't it," she asked Sam, already knowing the answer. Palmer picked up Tara and brought her over to Sam. He gently placed her on Sam's knee and sat down next to them on a log.

He placed his hand on her shoulder and squeezed gently. "Let's find a sunny spot where the ground won't be frozen, and we'll bury him. A proper funeral, for a hero," he added. Sam nodded.

Tara sniffled, looking up at her friends. "I know

the perfect place," she told them. "Next to the stream, where he protected me. There's a clearing there."

Together, they slowly gathered up their things and headed toward the stream. Sam carried the colander carefully. In the clearing, the rays of the sun had melted a large patch in the snow. Palmer dug a hole there with a big stick, and Sam gently lowered the brown rabbit into it. They covered him with soil and stones, and then searched for a larger rock to mark the place. Sam found a lovely one and rolled it onto the grave.

The three of them sat around it, Tara cradled in Sam's lap. After clearing her throat, Tara sang a beautiful song about the seasons. The melody was somber, but the words were not. They described the darkness of winter, and the promise of spring, year after year. Sam memorized the song, and hummed it all the way home.

FEBRUARY

The snow covering the ground had faded to a muddy gray. Sam looked out the window at the matching overcast sky. She hoped another snowfall would arrive to freshen up the dingy landscape. Its lack of color and tired appearance matched her mood.

The song of a cardinal interrupted the silence. Sam opened the window a crack to hear it, and searched the yard for the red bird. He sat in a holly bush, calling out to the windy woods. Sam watched him, and listened to his tune until the cold air chilled her, and she closed the window.

She glanced over at her work on the kitchen table. The sketches she had done in November for the Rawlings Conservation Fund were tacked up on the wall, and she was carefully creating large posters from the designs. Maddie was on her way over to help color in the lettering.

Sam sighed. Maddie was good company most of the time. But lately all she wanted to talk about was Palmer. She had a crush on him and was constantly giving Samantha notes to pass to him at school. Why didn't she just give them to him herself? Or text him?

Her eyes flickered over to her backpack on the kitchen table, which was filled with Maddie's tightly folded notes. Sam had let them pile up in there, undelivered. She felt a twinge of guilt and wondered why she hadn't given them to Palmer. Unzipping her backpack, she peered into it, and then looked away.

"Hey, Sam," Maddie hollered from the hallway, slamming the front door. Samantha jumped, and slid the backpack onto a chair.

"I'm in the kitchen!" she called out to Maddie, who strolled in with a bag from the craft store. She took off her coat and hung it over the chair, concealing the backpack. Sam gulped.

"I brought you some new markers and poster paint," Maddie smiled. Sam smiled back, her lips in a straight line, and sat down upon her backpack. It was a lumpy choice.

"Thanks," Sam replied, dumping the markers and paint out onto the table. "These are great. Mine were starting to dry out." She looked over at Maddie, admiring the sketches taped up on the wall.

"You're welcome," she replied, not taking her eyes off the drawings. "This one of the beech tree is amazing," she noted. "It kind of looks like it has a face, doesn't it?" She got up close and squinted at the paper. Sam hadn't noticed it, but the patterns in the bark on her drawings of the beech tree did look like eyes, a nose and a mouth. She got up to take a closer look.

Maddie linked her arm through Sam's. "Are these from photographs of a real tree, or did you make them up?" There were three drawings, but the patterns in the bark were the same on all of them.

"Not from photos," Sam answered. "It's a tree I've seen a lot, so it's clear in my mind, I guess."

Maddie nodded. "Maybe you could show me that tree sometime. It's really beautiful." She turned to Sam. "You're a great artist, Sam. I feel so lucky to be your friend."

Sam tightened her arm around Maddie's in a gentle squeeze. "Let's make some chocolate chip cookies and then finish up the posters," she suggested. The girls turned together toward the table, knocking Sam's backpack off the chair. Several of Maddie's notes spilled out, their tightly folded triangles tumbling onto the floor.

Sam's eyes grew wide as she reached for her backpack. Maddie beat her to it, and turned it upside down, shaking out books, pencils, a pack of gum, and half a dozen other notes. Several weeks worth of her efforts lay spread on the kitchen floor. She knelt down and started to gather them up in her shaking hands.

Sam knelt down next to her. "Maddie, I'm sorry I didn't get around to giving those to Palmer yet, but—"

Maddie cut her off. "Shut up, Sam." Her back was to her, hiding her face, but Sam could hear anger and pain mixed up in her voice. "All this time I thought he was a jerk, ignoring my questions. Turns out you're the jerk." Maddie stood up and grabbed the empty bag from the craft store and stuffed the notes into it.

Sam didn't know what to say. She opened her mouth, was about to lie, to tell Maddie that she'd planned to give them to Palmer but didn't want to unless he was alone, which he never was. The lie stuck in her throat and she closed her mouth. She looked away, unable to stand Maddie's eyes upon her.

"Really?" Maddie snapped. "Nothing to say?" Maddie looked down at Sam, still kneeling next to the table. "Thanks a lot," she said, grabbing her coat and stomping out of the kitchen. Sam flinched as the front door slammed shut.

The silence of the kitchen surrounded her. She lay down tiredly on the kitchen floor, listening for the cardinal, but he had gone. The clock ticked noisily from the hallway, and she focused on that for a few minutes.

Turning her head, she saw one of Maddie's

notes under the table. She rolled over and reached to get it. Stuffing it into her pocket, she stood up and exhaled a long breath. She grabbed her coat and headed outside.

The wind was blowing, and the light was fading. Among other things, Sam regretted not taking her hat and gloves. She zipped her coat up all the way and buried her hands in her pockets. She was so distracted by memories of Maddie's anger that she almost walked right into Palmer.

"Hey!" He stopped her with a hand out to her shoulder. "Where are you off to in such a hurry, and without watching where you're going? You almost walked right past me." Palmer tilted his head to one side and watched her. She felt a fresh wave of shame wash over her.

"Oh, hey yourself," she sniffed. "I was just coming over to give you this note from Maddie." She struggled to get at her back jeans pocket under her coat, and then handed the note to Palmer. He accepted it with a frown.

"Where are your gloves?" he asked, taking his own glove off to put the note in his pocket. "Do you want mine? It's freezing out here," he said, offering both his gloves in her direction. He was wearing a ski jacket and carrying an empty canvas bag.

"No thanks. Aren't you going to read it?" Sam asked. "I'm sure she would want you to read it right away. I think she wrote that a while ago." Her voice trailed off as she wiped her runny nose on her sleeve.

"I'll read it later," Palmer replied. "I was on my way to gather some firewood for the Woodlanders anyhow, they're running low. Want to join me? Two Protectlings can gather twice the wood in half the time, right?" He smiled at her. "I'm surprised you didn't get the message, too."

Sam was puzzled as well. It had been a few weeks since she'd gathered wood. Usually it was a weekly job this time of year. "Sure, but we'd better hurry. It'll be dark in about an hour."

The two of them sprinted back towards Sam's house and headed into the woods. On their way to the beech tree, they gathered sticks and twigs, filling the bag in short order.

It took some extra time to find and uncover the hatch. It was covered in snow and ice. Sam lowered herself down the ladder and got out of the way for Palmer. Once inside, they began unloading the canvas bag, breaking the sticks and twigs into smaller pieces for the Woodlanders to manage on their own. They stacked the wood carefully against the wall next to the corridor into the Great Hall.

"Is that you, Palmer?" Walter's voice echoed down the corridor. His shadow preceded him into the dimly lit area under the hatchway.

"And Samantha! Hello you two! Thank you for

bringing us more wood." Walter bowed in their direction. "Sam, it's good to see you. I wondered if you would make it this time, as you seem to have been unavailable recently?" Walter stepped toward her with questioning eyes.

"Unavailable?" Sam repeated. "I'm always available," she assured him.

Walter looked up at her. "The last few weeks we sent messages to both of you requesting a firewood run, but only Palmer responded. We thought perhaps you could not make it, which is fine. It is a busy time for you." Walter smiled patiently.

Sam was confused. Had she forgotten about the messages? Or did she not receive them? Usually they arrived in her dreams, and she woke up aware of the next job. She realized that she hadn't been aware of any requests for a few weeks now. Her eyes moved from Walter's face to Palmer's, and back again. The two of them shrugged at her. She searched Walter's face, but he turned away to gather an armful of wood. Palmer helped him load up the wheeled wood cart while Sam stood near the ladder, uncertain of what to do next.

Walter thanked them and headed into the Great Hall. Palmer made his way up the ladder, and Sam slowly made her way up behind him.

He reached down a hand to help her. "Maybe you didn't get the messages because you're sleeping too deeply," Palmer assured her. "My mom says it's gotten really hard to wake me up lately. I've been snoring through my alarm!" He laughed.

Sam didn't laugh. "That doesn't make any sense, Palmer," she whined. "Then you would have missed them too, and you haven't missed a single one." The two of them kicked a mess of snow, ice and dirt over the closed hatch.

"You've been really focused on the fair lately," Palmer added. "And your artwork. Maybe it's taking up all your dreams," he suggested.

Sam frowned at this. She felt perfectly capable of focusing on art and taking care of the Woodlanders at the same time. One shouldn't block out the other. Remembering the posters that needed to be finished, she picked up her pace.

She recalled the scene in the kitchen with Maddie. "Don't forget to read that note," Sam reminded him.

He jogged to keep up with her. "I'm sure it's just more questions," he said. "She wants to know what my favorite color is, my favorite sport, and candy. She's always texting me, too, but I'm not allowed to text friends, only Mom and Dad."

"Why don't you just answer her?" Sam wondered. It was unlike Palmer to be rude.

"I don't know," he replied. "Why don't you just tell her? You know all those things about me." He kicked at the snow as he walked. "I know your favorite color is blue, your favorite sport is football, and your favorite candy is gummy worms," Palmer added.

Sam smiled. She wanted to fix things with Maddie, but didn't know where to start. Part of her realized that she should tell Palmer about the other notes, but then she would have to explain why she hadn't given them to him. Since she couldn't find the words, she said nothing.

★ ★ ★

The next day in school, Sam waited by Maddie's locker between classes. Maddie had awkwardly avoided her on the morning bus. Sam took a deep breath as she saw Maddie stop a few feet away with a tired look on her face.

"Hey, Maddie," Sam met her halfway. "I know you don't want to talk to me, which I get, but I wanted to say I'm sorry," she reached out and put her hand on Maddie's arm. "I wasn't a good friend, and I hope you can forgive me."

Maddie pulled away, stepping around her to open her locker. She banged around in it, grabbing a book and putting a notebook inside before slamming it shut. When she turned around and saw Sam standing there, she rolled her eyes.

"I'm sorry, too, Sam." Maddie pouted. "I'm sorry that you like Palmer and were too wimpy to tell me, so you let me go on making a fool of myself for weeks, instead of being a good friend."

Maddie's words stung. Sam winced in silence as Maddie pushed past her down the crowded hall.

"Wait up, Maddie!" Sam called after her. Shuffling kids blocked her way, increasing the distance between her and Maddie. She scrambled to catch up, determined to get through to her. Boldly, she pushed her way through the crowd and stood her ground in front of Maddie, who stopped and sighed heavily.

"It's not like that," Sam insisted. Maddie glared at her, which rattled Sam's nerves. She felt her resolve weaken. For a second, she wanted to step aside and let Maddie go. It would be easier to give up.

Then she had an idea. Sam placed her hand on

her heart and focused on how much she really cared for Maddie. As she looked Maddie in the eye, the furrow in her friend's brow softened. A timid smile passed between them.

Maddie's shoulders relaxed, and she sighed heavily. "I'm still mad at you," she stated through pursed lips. "But, I accept your apology. You can make it up to me after school while we make some chocolate chip cookies and finish up the posters."

Sam nodded, linked her arm through Maddie's, and the two of them made their way down the hall in matching steps.

★　★　★

The fair was coming up in a few weeks, so they hung the posters up around town. A few went up at the high school, middle school, and Jared's elementary school. They put one in the Post Office and the drugstore as well. Grandpa Jack used the artwork in the email reminders that went out in the town e-newsletter. Palmer's mom paid Sam to make posters for the clothing drive, too, and wanted a few more to advertise the book sale at the town library. There was barely enough time to get her homework done.

There was a committee in charge of all the details for the Fun Fair. Sam's parents were on it, and they delegated all the art projects to the girls. The list of signs they needed seemed endless: Ticket

Booth, Refreshments, No Skateboarding, First Aid, Face Painting, Bake Sale, Fish Bowl Toss, Wacky Hair Booth. As soon as they finished some, there were more to make.

Lulu and Palmer were helping, too. They were in charge of designing and building the dunking booth. Lulu's Grandpa Martin and the twins worked on it with them. It wasn't going to be very warm in early March, so they were having trouble getting anyone to sign up to get dunked. Grandpa Jack agreed that they would do their best to make sure the water was warm. Palmer and Lulu both agreed to take a turn on the dunking seat.

Sam's parents were in charge of face painting. Sam signed up to spend a few hours working at their booth, as well as a few shifts making cotton candy. She was helping her parents print out face painting designs from the web when Palmer showed up at the back door. He waved at them through the glass.

"Come on in, Palmer," Sam's mom called across the room. He slid open the door and stepped into the kitchen. A blast of chilly air followed him. Sam's heart sank as she noticed the empty canvas bag he was carrying.

"Where're you off to, Palmer?" her dad asked over the noisy printer.

Palmer noticed Sam's eyes on the canvas bag and rolled it up, tucking it under his arm. "Just heading home, Mr. Penning. I wanted to check out the poster for the Dunk Tank, if Sam's finished it yet."

Sam nodded. "It's on the dining room table," she told him. He followed her into the next room. The two of them sifted through the large pile of posters.

"These look great," Palmer said. "I can't believe how many you've done."

Sam turned toward him. "Did you gather more wood just now, Palmer?" she whispered. He nodded slowly.

"Marta and Tom were there," he responded. "They asked where you were, and told me to let you know that it's okay if you don't have time for chores right now." Palmer squinted at her. "Did you not have time, or did you not get the message again?"

Sam exhaled. Every morning this week she had awakened thinking about the projects she needed to get done that day. Tasks from the Woodlanders were not on her to-do list. It didn't make any sense.

"Both, I guess," she answered. "I've been really busy, but their messages don't seem to be getting through to me. Maybe they've changed the way they send them or something." Sam looked at Palmer. "Does anything seem different to you?"

Palmer shook his head. "No, nothing is different. I just wake up some days thinking about what they need. Not everyday," he added. "It's okay, Sam. They don't seem to mind, so don't worry about it." He squeezed her shoulder, and headed into the kitchen.

Sam followed him to the door. He said goodbye to Mr. and Mrs. Penning, and gave Sam a reassuring smile. She tried to return it but could only manage a half-smile. She watched him walk off into the fading light of the evening.

That night before going to bed, Sam decided to take action. She wanted to improve any chances for messages to get through to her from the Woodlanders. After putting on her pajamas and brushing her teeth, she gathered up her sketchbooks. She brought them into bed with her and flipped through them, remembering the events that their pages illustrated. The Lamp Lighting, the Amber Token, drawings of the beech tree in different seasons ...

One of them captured her attention, and she studied it closely. It was the one of the raccoon family, the little ones clustered around their mother among the ferns. She remembered how she had held her hand over her heart to connect with the mother raccoon. Then she thought of the moment in the hallway at school with Maddie, when she had been able to communicate her feelings to her friend without words. Maddie seemed to get the message loud and clear.

MARCH

Samantha loved the beginning of spring. It was still chilly, but little green sprouts began peeking out of the soil. Patches of purple and white crocuses bloomed next to the house where the dryer vent blew out warm air. Yellow-green buds emerged on the trees, and the air smelled clean.

The Fun Fair was planned for Saturday. Sam, Palmer, Maddie and Lulu got off the bus at the high school after school on Friday to help set up. Rain was in the forecast, so the fair was going to take place in the field house instead of outside. Mr. MacKenzie was unhappy about this, but Grandpa Jack assured him that it would still go well. The four kids found them arguing by the door.

"Just a few rain showers," Jack said to Martin. "The field house looks like a big-top circus tent! Couldn't be more perfect. Sam here can decorate the doors to look like tent flaps." Jack turned to Sam with a hopeful smile.

Sam didn't miss a beat. "Absolutely, we can do that," she answered. "Hang some fabric and brightly colored pennant banners ..."

Martin frowned and folded his arms. "Fine," he said, resigned. "Get started on that. Let us know what you need for supplies and I'll run out and get them."

The kids worked wonders with what he brought them. The doors to the field house did look like the entrance to a circus tent, with blue bed sheets, rope, and strings of rainbow pennant banners. Someone added a red carpet and velvet ropes from the drama department. Dozens of helium balloons would be added in the morning.

Sam's posters went up at each station. The ticket booth was near the entrance, and the rest of the booths were set up in a balanced fashion around the huge space. Everything looked ready to go by the end of the afternoon, with all hands chipping in for a final cleanup and sweeping.

That night, Sam was too excited to sleep. She lay in bed, looking forward to painting faces and trying some goodies from the bake sale. She started to doze off as she imagined rows of cupcakes with sprinkles.

A noise at her window startled her. It sounded as if a pebble or nut bounced against the glass. She pulled back the covers and padded quietly over to check it out. As she approached the window, an acorn pinged the glass, answering at least part of her query. She opened it, and stuck her head out into the cool night air.

"Hey," someone whispered from the shadows below. It was Palmer. She couldn't see him, but she recognized his voice. "Meet me at the gate!" She heard him run in that direction.

Had she forgotten something? Or missed another message from the Woodlanders? Palmer seemed calm, so that was good. It didn't sound like anything alarming. Her heart raced as she quickly threw on a sweatshirt and jeans, and grabbed her sneakers. In a few moments she was down her ladder and across the grass. She braided her hair into a single plait down her back on the way.

Palmer was leaning against one of the stone posts of the gate. Tara sat on it, whispering to Palmer. As Sam got closer, she noticed Marta and Tom perched on the other post. They all greeted her in hushed excitement.

"Is everything alright?" she murmured. She could see them nodding now that her eyes had adjusted to the dark.

Tara leaned toward her, "Couldn't be better! We wanted you to join us on an adventure—last minute plans! Palmer's idea, really, but it has to be tonight!"

She took a step toward Palmer. He looked up toward the house, and then bent his head closer toward hers to fill her in on the details. The Woodlanders were excited to hear about the Fun

Fair, and they wanted to see it all. It wouldn't be safe for them to go in daylight, and tomorrow everything would be taken down and cleaned up before dark. So, he had offered to give them a pre-opening, nighttime tour of the field house.

Sam listened and shook her head. "That's crazy! Are you going to break in? It's locked and …"

The sound of keys jingling stopped her protest. Palmer returned them to his pocket.

"You stole those?" Her voice rose above a whisper and Tom and Marta hushed her gently.

"I borrowed them, from my Mom's purse, just for an hour or so," Palmer explained. "We'll be back before anyone wakes up. They just want to have a look."

Marta addressed Sam. "Of course, you don't have to join us. We will understand completely if you want to stay behind."

A long moment passed while Sam sighed with uncertainty. She seemed to be the only one who thought this was a bad idea. It would also be really fun, and she didn't want to miss it.

"I'm in," she decided. "Let's get going—it'll take a few hours to see the place and get you three back to the homestead, and it's already 12:30."

Small claps sounded from her friends' little hands. Palmer and Sam lifted them from the posts and placed them gently in the grass. The tiny family jogged behind Palmer, and Sam followed carefully.

Soon the lights of the field house parking lot glowed ahead of them.

Palmer sprinted ahead to unlock the door. He had brought a flashlight, and flicked it on and off in their direction. The four of them made their way to join him, careful to stay in the shadows. He ushered them inside and closed the heavy, metal door.

It was dark except for the glowing exit signs. Six of them made it easy enough to see, so Palmer didn't need his flashlight. They stood looking around for a moment and caught their breath.

Palmer took a few steps toward the nearest booth. "This is where tickets are sold for all the activities," he explained. "Four tickets for face painting, three for fortune telling, two for crafts and games, and six for the Dunk Tank."

The Woodlanders were curious about the dunk tank. Someone paid to throw a ball at a target to plunge a friend into water? They wanted to see it.

They made their way toward the far end of the field house, where the dunk tank was set up next to the trophy case. On the way, Palmer pointed out Sam's posters. They stopped in front of a large one of the beech tree.

"Preserve, Conserve, Protect," read Tara. "It's beautiful, Sam!" The family looked up at it, squinting in the dim light. Palmer turned on his flashlight and focused its beam, so that they could see better.

Marta sighed and tilted her head. "You captured our home perfectly, Sam. I'm so impressed with your work." Tom and Tara agreed. Sam thanked them, and offered to pass it along to them after the fair.

They moved on to the dunk tank. Palmer and Sam were surprised to find it already filled with water.

"I guess your grandpa wanted the water to warm up a little," Palmer figured. "So you won't get chilled when I dunk you," he added.

"You're the one who's getting dunked!" Sam shoved him without much force.

"If you're so sure I can't sink you, let's give our friends a little demonstration," Palmer challenged.

Sam looked at the tank. It was about six feet tall and four feet wide. Half of it was filled with water, and a slim bench was positioned near the top. A small ladder on the back provided entrance for the fall guy, or girl. Extending from one side, a red target stuck out, attached to a spring under the water that released the bench. The target was the size and shape of a dinner plate. Two large baskets stood nearby—one filled with India red rubber balls and the other with towels.

Sam smiled. "Okay, you get three tries. When you fail, it'll be my turn, and we can show them how that spring mechanism collapses the bench and dumps you into the water."

"Deal," Palmer agreed. "Ladies first." He walked over to the trophy case and removed a large one. It was the perfect height to nestle the flashlight on, so it illuminated the center of the tank. Sam bowed in the spotlight and turned to climb the ladder. She stepped onto the bench, sat down, and dangled her feet in the water. It wasn't very warm, and she shivered for a second.

Marta, Tom and Tara watched next to the trophy as Palmer retrieved a ball from the basket. He positioned himself behind the yellow line of tape on the floor in front of the tank.

"Are - you - ready?" he whispered, loud enough for all of them to hear. Sam signaled with a nod, and he whipped the ball as hard as he could at the target. Sam closed her eyes and held on tightly to the bench. She heard the rubber ball hit the wall behind her with a smack.

Laughter and claps erupted from the Woodlanders, and a groan of defeat from Palmer followed. He ran after the ball and resumed his position behind the line.

"Now I'm warmed up," he warned Sam. She closed her eyes again, but relaxed on the bench. Palmer focused his aim, and sent the ball directly into the target. A bell rang, and the bench collapsed under her. She hit the water fast and tumbled to the bottom of the tank. She knelt there and pressed her hands against the front of the tank and made a silly face at her little friends.

They laughed and clapped again, and Palmer bowed in their direction. They pointed at the silly faces Sam was making under the water.

Sam turned to stand, but something caught at her braid. The top of her head was only an inch from the surface of the water, but she couldn't stand up. Her braid was stuck in the spring. She pulled with all her might, but it wouldn't release. She tried to scream and only large bubbles came out instead. She banged on the tank as hard as she could.

"Something's wrong!" Palmer raced over, climbed the ladder and jumped into the tank. He tried to pull her out, but her hair was caught on something. He kicked at the side of the tank, knowing that he would have to break it somehow, and fast. Just then, something hit against the outside of the tank. The Woodlanders had struggled to push the trophy over, and they were trying to lift it.

Palmer bounded up the ladder and fell over the side. The Woodlanders scattered out of his way. He slipped and fell scrambling to get the trophy. In one quick motion, he picked it up and swung it like a bat against the side of the tank. It bounced off, and he swung again, to no avail. The Woodlanders had run over to the basket, and were wringing their hands.

"There's a bigger one in the case!" Tara yelled to Palmer. He dropped the trophy and ran over to the display case, frantically grabbing at a heavier one with a marble base. He dragged it over to the tank and swung again.

The stone base cracked against the tank but didn't break it. His next swing lodged the trophy in a hole it created, and he wrenched it free with all the strength he had left. Water rushed out, and Sam was able to gulp some air as the level dropped a few inches. It continued to drain out around Palmer's feet. He dropped the trophy and fell onto his knees, breathing heavily.

The Woodlanders rushed over, splashing in the streams of water. Sam looked at them, wide-eyed and sputtering. "My braid is stuck," she wheezed. She sat down in the tank. The hole had let out half the water, but it was still up to her chest. She reached over and tugged at her braid.

Palmer crawled over to join them. "Are you okay?" When she nodded at him, he sat back heavily against the tank and closed his eyes for a second.

Marta pressed her hands against the tank. "We are going to get you out of there, Sam."

"This dunk tank is the worst!" Tara stomped hard in a puddle. "Where is the craft table? We need some scissors."

Palmer stood up and headed to find some. Tom went over to the basket and pulled down a towel. It fell onto the wet ground and became instantly soaked.

After a few minutes, Palmer returned with a pair of scissors. He climbed the ladder and jumped in, kneeling next to Sam.

He looked her in the eye. "Sorry I have to cut your braid off."

Sam assured him that she was ready, and he chopped away at it. It took a few tries, but soon she was released and stood up, stretching her legs and arms. She climbed slowly up the ladder and joined the Woodlanders in a dry spot near the trophy case. Palmer worked a few more minutes with the scissors and got most of her braid out of the spring. A piece of it was still stuck there, and the bench couldn't be reset.

"It's no use, Palmer." Tom had looked around for some other tools. "There's no fixing it, or repairing that hole. I think it is an unsafe attraction, and the fair will be better off without it."

Sam looked down at her wet braid in her hand. She and Palmer dried up the floors as best they could, and put the trophies and balls away. Still, it was a disaster. They needed to lock up and get the Woodlanders back to the beech tree.

The five of them trudged toward the door. Their shoes squeaked, and their clothes dripped. Palmer and Sam each had a towel around their shoulders.

Marta cleared her throat. "I am so sorry things

turned out the way they did tonight. We are so grateful that you are okay, Sam, and nothing else matters."

Palmer thanked them for their quick thinking. He told them that he hadn't thought to use the trophy to crack the tank. It was a brilliant idea.

His house was right next to the field house, but he wanted to walk with Sam all the way to the beech tree so that they could agree on a plan. They decided that they would have to come up with a complicated lie, and it would take some rehearsing to get all the details straight. They might have to stay up all night.

On the walk back, they worked out a story about how someone must have stolen the keys and broken in during the night. Sam and Palmer could go early and say that they found the door open and the dunk tank all busted, but no sign of who did it. And Sam had fallen asleep with gum in her mouth, and it had gotten stuck in her hair, so she had to cut it off ...

By the time they got to the beech tree, it seemed as if all the details were straight. Marta and Tom had remained silent. Tara asked her parents what they thought of the plan.

Tom stopped at the roots of the tree and sat down in the darkness. It would be light in an hour or so, and the sky was losing its blackness already. "It is a clever story," he nodded to them. "It is obvious that you cannot tell your parents that you were bringing tiny people who live in the woods to see the Fun Fair. This would jeopardize the safety of all the Woodlanders. However, I would encourage you to tell the truth about the rest of what happened."

Sam and Palmer looked at each other. "I don't get how that would work at all," Sam whined. Their clothes had dried a bit on the walk. They sat down on some soft moss.

Marta leaned toward them. "If you take responsibility for your actions, it will be difficult. You will suffer the consequences, which will be unpleasant. Your parents love you very much. Still, they will be angry with you, and hurt by your disrespect of their rules. It will take some time for them to trust you again."

Palmer blinked at her. "Right, exactly. That's why we have to lie, to avoid all that." Tara studied Palmer's face. He was blinking a lot. He continued, "It's not our fault. It's your fault. You asked to see the Fun Fair. We wouldn't have gone if you hadn't asked us to."

"It is no one's fault, Palmer," Tom added, gently. "It was an accident. Blaming is not constructive. I am sorry our request ended up in a messy situation, but it will be okay. Lying about what happened will only add to the mess. It will also require you to tell other lies every day, and your mind will not be peaceful."

"The consequences I mentioned are things you can handle," Marta told them. "Especially if you face them directly, together. This would include asking your parents for forgiveness, and telling them you are sorry."

Tom looked at their doubtful expressions. "We understand that being a Protectling requires a lot of secrecy," he said. "But we hope you can see the difference between protecting the safety of others, and lying to protect yourself."

No one spoke. Tara yawned and stretched. "I'm so glad that you are alright, Sam. That was terrifying! I'm exhausted and you guys must be, too." She looked up at her friends. "Palmer, you are so strong and brave. I'm glad you take care of us all so well. Thank you." She blew them kisses and disappeared into the roots of the tree.

Marta and Tom stood up to follow her. Marta sighed heavily. "I have faith in you both," she told them, placing her hand over her heart. Tom did the same, and they retired to their rest.

Palmer and Sam looked at each other. They turned to find the trail, and headed home with heavy steps.

★   ★   ★

The Fun Fair raised over four thousand dollars for the Conservation Fund. The busted dunk tank was pushed into a corner and covered up with some sheets. Most of the people who came to the fair didn't know there was going to be a dunk tank, so it wasn't really missed. Palmer and Sam had agreed to tell their parents that he had borrowed the keys, and that they had snuck into the field house after dark to try out the tank, and that Sam's braid had gotten stuck and Palmer had to crack the tank with a trophy to save her. Everyone was so relieved that Sam was alive and not drowned, they couldn't be too mad at them. They were each grounded for three weeks and not allowed any screen time, except for one hour on Saturdays. They were both given extra chores as well.

On the walk home after leaving the beech tree, they had agreed to wake their parents up early and tell the truth, as best they could, without including the Woodlanders.

Palmer asked her how it went, while she painted a trophy on his cheek at the face-painting booth. She applied a final dab of gold paint, and some white highlights.

"I was really nervous," she told him, as she painted a few drops of water dripping from the trophy. "They were pretty shocked that you stole the keys, so that took some focus off me. I assured them that you weren't in the habit of stealing stuff."

"Thanks." Palmer accepted the hand mirror she offered him and checked out his face. He couldn't decide on a design, and had told her to pick something. He was pleased. "Here," he said, handing back the mirror. "You need this. Your hair looks terrible." They laughed. Sam's mom had done a decent job of tidying up a chin-length bob, and it looked fine.

"How'd it go with your parents?" Sam looked at her short hair in the mirror, and sighed.

"My dad told me that it'll take a long time for him to trust me again, and then he told me that I'm a hero. So I guess it could be worse. And my mom cried."

"Ugh, I hate it when they cry." Sam rolled her eyes. She caught sight of Lulu and Maddie heading their way.

"Is it true?" Lulu pounced on them. "You two are grounded for smashing the dunk tank? My brother and sister worked so hard on that—they're gonna kill you!" Palmer and Sam were not worried about Lulu's gentle siblings.

Maddie had missed the story, so Palmer filled her in on the details, and the girls admired Sam's new haircut as evidence. The four of them shared some cupcakes on their break, and worked hard the rest of the day.

That night, Sam fell asleep on top of her comforter with her clothes still on. She slept for twelve hours, not waking up even when the scent of waffles drifted upstairs.

★   ★   ★

Sam's dad kept a list of what he called 'fair-weather projects'—a large number of jobs around the house and in the yard to be tackled on spring weekends. Everyone was expected to chip in and help. Sam still had extra chores from the dunk tank mess. The work usually started out with complaints from Sam and Jared, but ended with everyone in good spirits around the dinner table.

Their house had been built in the 1960s. Samantha's mom had grown up there on Primrose Lane. After she got married, Grandpa Jack and Gram Ellen sold her the house and bought a condo in the city.

Grandpa Jack and his friend, Martin, were the developers who planned the neighborhood, and were the first ones to move in. Together they ran the Rawlings Meadow Conservation Commission, which kept any other developers from building in the woods.

Her mom loved the place. She enjoyed sharing childhood memories of forts and hideouts with Sam and Jared. Aunt Beth and Sam's mother had a playroom in the attic back then, but now it was filled with junk. This weekend's project included a spring-cleaning of the attic.

"Sam, please bring up some empty laundry baskets and black trash bags from downstairs," her mom called from the second floor landing. Her dad was already up the narrow steps, changing the light bulbs in the attic. Jared was helping him by steadying the ladder. Samantha had trouble getting the wide baskets up the cramped stairway. Her mother followed closely behind, carrying a broom and dustpan.

"Yuck! It smells horrible up here. So musty." Sam crinkled her nose and stuck out her tongue at Jared. He plugged his nose. Sam put down the baskets and headed over to the far end of the attic to open a window.

She would have loved this space as a playroom, but her dad thought it was too dangerous. Comments were made about how irresponsible her grandparents had been to let two little girls play up here, with unstable flooring and rusty nails poking out of the woodwork.

The window at the end of the attic was covered with dust and the remains of an old wasp's nest. It opened easily, and cool air rushed in. Sam leaned her head out to soak up the green smells. The view into the woods was fresh for her—different from the one she enjoyed from her bedroom window. She could see the tops of the trees in the woods. Off in the distance, the crown of the great beech was visible above its younger neighbors. It was speckled with yellow-green buds.

"Sam, why don't you start by cleaning out this

old dresser?" her mom asked. "The drawers are filled with old books and toys. See what should be given to Goodwill and put the rest in a garbage bag."

Sam stepped away from the window and took the bag from her mom. The dresser had four sagging drawers. The first one was packed with faded comic books. "Don't throw those away!" Jared bounded over, examining the pile Sam was heaping on the floor. He knelt over them and grabbed one off the top.

The next drawer was more interesting. Within it sat a fat notebook and two old cigar boxes. Their tops were decorated with moss and twigs, and dried globs of glue. Samantha picked one up and showed it to her mother. "Mom, did you make this?"

Her mom dropped the broom and reached for the box with a smile. "No, Aunt Beth made that. It's a treasure box." She lifted its lid and examined the contents: painted acorns and stones, a few feathers, some crumbled bracelets made out of dried flowers.

Sam picked up the notebook and admired page after page of beautiful pencil drawings. No color, just silvery gray etchings of trees and streams, and some close up studies of leaves and rocks. She froze, wide-eyed, on a page in the middle. It was a sketch of her beloved beech tree. The drawing was a careful one, detailing moss and roots. She couldn't look away from it.

"Is there another box like this one?" her mother interrupted. "I made one too, I remember." Sam peeked into the drawer and lifted out the second box. It was similarly adorned with brown bits from the forest. Inside were the same treasures, plus a few other trinkets collected in play.

Sam blinked hard and noticed her mom pick up a beechnut and turn it over in her hand. She put it back, and then took out a frayed bit of cloth from the box and brought it over to the window to look at it in the sunlight.

"I wonder what this is..." She pondered it, turning over the fabric in her hand. "I think I made it, but I can't remember. It's pretty! I think it's a small part of a bigger piece." She placed it on top of the dresser and went back to the painted stones in the box.

Samantha recognized the braided pattern immediately and grabbed it. Upon closer inspection she was sure of it: tattered and discolored with age, it was a piece from a braided ladder identical to the one she had made herself. She gulped, and her mind started spinning. Had her mother made this? Other questions pin-balled around her mind, so fast she couldn't process them. She felt unsteady and had to sit down on the floor.

Glancing up at her mother, Sam became alarmed. Her mom closed the box, and picked up the notebook. Sam watched her flip though it, close it and then reach for the broom.

"Mom, wait," Samantha jumped up to stand in front of her mother, holding out the braided piece. "You made this?" she asked her, not wanting to hear the answer.

"I think so," she replied. "I do remember making it, sort of, but I don't recall when, or where the rest of it went. Although I'm pretty certain it's part of a bigger braid." Sam's hands began to tingle. She'd been holding her breath.

"Sam, what's wrong?" Her mother reached out to her, but Sam backed away. "Honey, I think Sam needs some fresh air. She looks sick or something." Her mom's worried face swam before Sam's eyes.

Then she yelled at her mother, "What do you mean you don't remember? You're lying!" Her mother stared blankly back at her. Sam batted her father's hands away as he stepped toward her. She stood between them, feeling her neck redden. Her knees were shaking.

The look on her mother's face told her what she didn't want to know: that she had made a ladder just like Sam's, and that now she had no idea what it was. It didn't mean anything to her. Marta and Tom had told Sam. No grown-ups were Protectlings. Her mother had been one, just like Sam. And now she had forgotten all about it? It was a nightmare. Samantha would not allow this to happen to her.

"Sweetie, let's go downstairs and get you some water. I think you must be coming down with a virus or something." Her mom reached for her again.

"Don't touch me!" Sam hollered. Jared sat wide-eyed on the floor, neglecting the comic books. He thought Sam looked like she was about to cry.

"How could you be so stupid!" She yelled at her mother.

"Honey, what's wrong?" her mother asked.

"Be careful!" Her parents tried to stop her from bounding down the attic stairs, but it was too late. Samantha was through the next flight of stairs and out the back door in an instant, running for the woods.

Her parents looked at each other. "Should I go after her?" her father asked. They watched from the attic window as she ran into the woods.

Her mom shook her heard. "No, I think she needs a little time to herself. She's been so moody lately."

"I'm sure she'll get hungry for lunch soon and head home," he promised her. They gave each other a reassuring hug and got back to work.

Her mom bent to pick up the flannel braid Sam had dropped near the stairs. It was just an old scrap from some craft project, long ago. She wondered why it had made Sam so upset. She remembered being awful to her own mother at that age. As she fingered the fabric, she sighed. It made her feel better to hold it, so she tucked it into her pocket. She looked out the window at the treetops and hoped that Sam was finding some quiet there.

★　★　★

Outside, Sam ran until she was out of breath. She fell onto her knees in a batch of soft ferns and started to sob heavily. Her chest hurt. Wiping her runny nose on the front of her shirt, she stood up and took some deep breaths. She had run right past the spot on the trail that led to the homestead, so she backtracked to find it. It took her awhile. Nothing felt familiar to her.

Coming up with a plan was not easy. She was having trouble thinking clearly. She wanted to find Tom and Marta. They would be happy to see her and would promise that nothing would change. She could go on being a Protectling forever.

Her feet dragged through pine needles, and she tripped on a tree root. Instead of getting up, she stayed where she had fallen, sitting back and crossing her legs. The giant beech stood up ahead, welcoming her. Warm breezes rustled through its branches. She studied some nuthatches playing there, singing noisily.

The tree seemed to be breathing. Her love for this place, the living friend in front of her, was limitless. No more tears came. Her own breath slowed in rhythm with the movement of the branches above her, creating a calmness that poured over her whole body.

She watched the tree for a long time. The light changed around her while she listened to the birds and chipmunks. From where she had landed when she tripped, she scooted closer to the tree, nestling into a space between its roots. The questions that troubled her were fading from her mind. They were replaced by other questions: What would her summer be like? What important things would she do in her life? She wanted to take that class at Westley College for kids called *So You Want To Be An Innovator* with Maddie. She would have to choose between that and Camp Walden soon.

Sam knew that she didn't need to worry about the Woodlanders. They would be safe. There were many Protectlings. Oliver and Paige would be among them when they got older. She would honor the order of things. This is what she had learned from them. Caring for them meant walking away, and becoming what she was meant to be next. Whatever that was. It did not include any responsibilities in these woods.

Sam was exhausted. Running and crying had left her drained and sleepy. She wiped her damp cheeks on her sleeve and yawned. Lying down seemed very appealing. A mossy patch next to the tree looked like a pillow to her sleepy eyes, so she rested her head there. She drifted off and fell into dreams of warm breezes carrying her above the treetops. In her dream she viewed the woods from an outlook high in the beech tree, where she could see the stream in the distance and hear it gurgling.

The sun passed overhead and the shadows grew longer. A rumbling in Sam's stomach awakened her. She stood up slowly, stretching her arms above her head.

"I'm hungry," she said out loud, to no one. Then she recalled the quarrel with her mother in the attic and felt ashamed. She wanted to apologize and vowed to be kinder. More than anything, she wanted to be back there now, with her family, doing her share of the work. She reached over to the beech tree and brushed her hand along its beautiful bark before looking for the trail. It was around here somewhere, although she could not remember in which direction. She looked right, then left, then spotted it, directly in front of her. She made her way to it and headed home, glancing once over her shoulder before looking back no more.

Our story continues in …

THE
PROTECTLINGS
On the Common

ACKNOWLEDGMENTS

It took a long time to complete this book, and I could not have done it without help from my early readers. I'm grateful for their time and invaluable input: Melissa Bowyer, Roberta Carr, Claire DeLandro, Sharon Felzer, George and Wenda Gantz, Michelle Hackenson, Tess Heilman, Eamonn Keating, Chuck Kerber, Karla Kloc, Joan Lynch, Freya Pendleton, Katherine Pikulik, Juliette Smith, Kerry Stratton, and Cathy Toran. Carol Callahan was my insightful and diligent editor. Erika Kurtiak Heilman was generous with her publishing expertise.

This story is based on ones my daughters told as children exploring the woods, so I must thank them for much of the imagery. Both of them are brilliant storytellers.

Special thanks go to my brother, Chaz. His steady encouragement fueled me on many days when my tank was empty.

The Protectlings would not have seen the light of day without the unflagging support of my writing partner and kindred spirit, Leah Carey. Our weekly meetings inspired me in countless ways, in all areas of my life. Leah's wisdom and guidance pried me out of stuck spaces over and over. Her wonderful husband, Carl Scholz, helped me format each page. This book looks the way it does because of his painstaking efforts to bring it all together.

I'm blessed to be married to my best friend. I want to thank my beloved Carl for being a constant source of peace and comfort for me. His boundless interest in nature impacted this story on many levels. Our connection is the cornerstone of my reverence and wonder for the world.

ABOUT THE AUTHOR

Carolyn Heilman lives outside of Boston with her husband, on the edge of protected public woodlands. Nature inspires her, so she tries to spend time each day walking in the woods in every season. Writing, drawing and oil painting are her favorite creative pursuits. Carolyn's love of books and stories has been a constant delight since her earliest memories. She is a devoted literacy tutor and former teacher.

More of Carolyn's thoughts on books and writing can be found at her website, The Mandala Writers Circle, www.mandalawriterscircle.com.

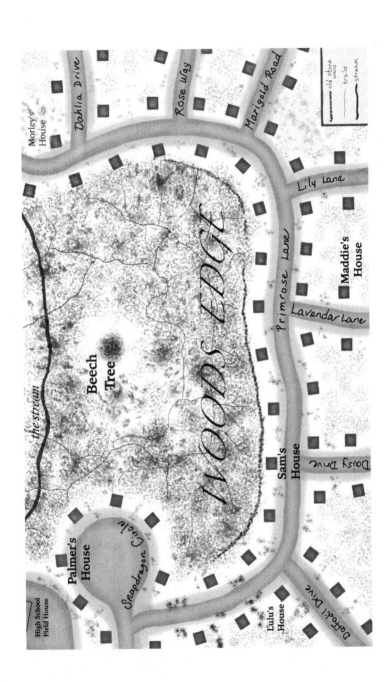